RAZOR'S RETURN

RAZOR'S RETURN

by

Kimberly A. Biggerstaff

Cover art by

Ivan Zanchetta & Bookcoversart.com

Paperback ISBN: 979-8-9900297-5-0

KAB-BAK Co.

Novels by Kimberly A. Biggerstaff

A Rogov Romance

Lex's Story

Lex's Story Part II: Life Unguarded

Love at the Pentagon: A Nick & Gia Story

Love at Haily's Comet

The Sam Barrett Ops: The Missions

Operation: Princess

Other novellas and novels by Alex A. Jameson

(Kimberly A. Biggerstaff)

The Sam Barrett Ops

Operation: Running Brook

Operation: Russian Roulette

Operation: Returning Home

Operation: Rising Son

Operation: Payback

Operation: Rescue Requited

Operation: Birdwatcher

Operation: Cougar

Operation: Breakdown

Operation: Newcomer

Operation: Dagger Heart

Operation: Throat Punch

Operation: Angel Heart

This page left blank

This page left blank

DEDICATION

To all American Legion posts around the world, especially my friends at C. M. Joslin Post 618 in Willis, Texas, and my home post, The Woodlands Post 305, The Woodlands, Texas.

Thank you for all you do for our veterans and their families.

Thank you to my family for putting up with this new hobby.

Thank you to my sister-in-law, Stephanie Thompson.

Thanks to all who have encouraged me, including my grandmother, Cretora Biggerstaff.

CHAPTER 1

Razor waited around until he was assigned to a golfer. He had volunteered to caddy at the charity golf tournament to get in some community service. It was for a good cause, and it would also be a relaxing way to spend a day off.

"Next," a woman called from behind a table.

Razor stepped up, and the woman gave him a look like she thought he was in the wrong place. "Reston. I'm here to caddy."

She looked at her list. "Reston. Yes, you'll be with Eve Patterson. Thank you for volunteering today." She handed him a scorecard and two pencils.

"Yes, ma'am. No problem," he said.

"Miss Patterson is over there." She pointed to a woman dressed in a Ralph Lauren polo shirt, matching golf skort, and visor. Her light-brown hair was pulled back into a neat ponytail under her visor. She was talking to some other golfers.

As he walked to her, he couldn't help but glance at her legs. *Nice.* "Miss Patterson, I'm your caddy," Razor said. When she turned around, his heart skipped a beat. The air in his lungs suddenly disappeared. It was like in training, when he was underwater and the instructor messed with his diving gear.

They'd do things like tie your hoses in knots. You needed to remain calm and work the problem. He took in a slow deep breath. She was beautiful. Then he realized he was staring. *Big ape, pull it together. She's probably married to a guy here.*

She smiled and said, "Great. Let's go. What's your name?"

"Uh—"

Before he could answer, a voice over the loudspeaker said, "Team Patterson, head to the tee area. Team Patterson."

"That's us. Come on. My clubs are outside," she told him.

Razor followed the team and other caddies like a dutiful soldier—or sailor, as the case may be. It wasn't difficult to figure out which golf bag was hers. It was a red, white, and blue Callaway golf bag with her name embroidered on it. *Ralph Lauren clothes and Callaway golf equipment. Too classy.* He picked up the bag and followed everyone to the first tee.

*****

Eve Patterson had been golfing well all day. Her mixed team of two men and two women was in second place by one stroke. Approaching the sixteenth hole, she glanced at her caddy and asked for a club. He had been quiet the entire day and had handed her the club she requested without question—until now. This time he hesitated.

"Excuse me? Could I have the eight, please?" she asked, thinking he hadn't heard her.

"Seven iron, ma'am," he said in a deep, gruff voice.

"I asked for an eight, please," she said, looking up at the large man.

"You'll be short."

"What are you talking about?" Eve was a very good golfer and what was known as a scratch golfer. She could score par or better on every hole. But everyone made mistakes and although she'd played this course before, they'd done some landscaping and changed the course slightly since the last time she'd played.

He showed her the scorecard. He'd written down each club she'd used and the distance she'd shot. "A seven will put you on the green," he said.

Impressed with his reasoning, she took the seven iron, and her shot landed inches from the hole. She handed him the club, smiled, and said, "Thank you." Walking to the green, Eve thought about her caddy. He looked slightly out of place, and she wondered about him.

"Eve, your shot," one of her teammates said.

She approached her ball but was suddenly aware of her caddy watching her. She took a deep breath and cleared her head. Eve took a practice swing with her putter and lined up her shot. It was an easy three-inch putt. Or it should have been, but this man kept invading her thoughts. She silently talked herself into a state of concentration. She cleared her throat, took another breath, drew the putter back, and sank the ball into the cup. She birdied the last two holes to finish two strokes off her personal best. Eve high-fived her teammates, and they made their way toward the clubhouse. She was happy with her performance, and her team finished the tournament in second place, although first place would have been better. She was a little competitive.

"You can set my bag there. Thank you," Eve told her caddy. He did so and handed her the scorecard. She looked it over and signed it, but when she glanced up, he was gone. Walking into the clubhouse, she handed in her scorecard and went to get a drink. Taking a sip of her wine, she turned and saw her caddy drinking a beer alone at a small table. Wanting to find out more about this man, she started to approach him but was stopped as the presentation of trophies commenced. Eve waited, and when her team was called, they went up and received their trophy. After all the obligatory congratulations were finished, she looked at the table and was glad he was still there.

"Thank you for your help today," she said, standing next to his table with her glass of wine.

Not expecting anyone to talk to him, he stood up and looked around. "Um, yes, ma'am. No problem."

"Are you waiting for someone?" she asked, not wanting to impose.

"No, ma'am."

"May I join you?" she asked.

"Excuse me?"

She chuckled. "May I sit down and join you?"

"Yes, ma'am."

She smiled. "I'm sorry, but I don't think I got your name. I'm Eve," she said, setting her second place trophy on the table. She was embarrassed that she had played the entire day without knowing his name. She extended her hand.

"Razor," he said quickly, shaking her hand and sitting back down.

"Good. Now please stop calling me ma'am. Razor? That sounds more like a nickname. Let me guess: It has something to do with your beard," she said. He was dressed appropriately in golf slacks and a polo, but his very thick, slightly long beard was out of place. So was his ball cap, which had a patch with a skull on it commonly known as the Punisher.

"Yes," he said.

"Is there another name I can call you?"

"No." He shifted slightly in his seat.

She smiled again. "Is it an embarrassing name?"

"No."

"OK," she said, giving up. He seemed like a quiet man. Quite the opposite of what she thought someone of his size would be like. "What do you do when you aren't volunteering at golf tournaments, Razor?"

"Navy."

"That makes sense." She elaborated when he raised an eyebrow. "Your hat and the tattoo peeking out from under your shirtsleeve made me think you're military. You must be on leave with that beard." She took a sip of her wine. "Or you're special warfare. An operator. I didn't think operators were as big as you are." Razor was a large man at six foot five and 275 pounds of muscle. Although he was over the weight limit for naval standards, he was under the body fat percentage for his age, and he always scored in the excellent range for his physical readiness test.

He stared at her blankly. *Special warfare? That wasn't what someone typically said unless they had some knowledge of the navy.*

A man walked by and smiled at Eve. "Nice play today, Eve."

"Thanks, Don." She returned her attention to Razor. "Not much of a talker, are you?"

"No." He took a sip of his beer. He never spoke much unless he needed to. Combat was different for this seasoned, disciplined operator. As the second ranked enlisted man on the team, he barked out orders when necessary. Razor was known for keeping his cool under pressure and getting the job done. When all hell would break loose, Razor was there for his team, and when one of them got hit during an op, Razor carried him to safety, held his hand, and talked to him until the man drew his last breath. It was one of the few things that still haunted him.

Eve noticed that he kept looking around. "Are you sure you aren't waiting for someone?"

"Only your boyfriend or husband."

"I'm not married, and I don't have a boyfriend." She smiled again at him. "You know, if I'd have used the eight, I would have come up short, and we would have taken third. Do you play golf?"

"Not really. Just mess around."

"You should. Maybe we could play sometime," she said, raising the glass of wine to her lips as Razor watched.

*****

As they sat at the table, a tournament official approached Eve. "Excuse me, Eve. You won the Senator's Cup today. We need to do another presentation." He let out a sigh of relief. "I was afraid you'd left."

"Is that something new, George?" she asked.

"Yes. The Senator's Cup is for the best female score, and the Governor's Cup is for the best male. Congratulations. You won by one stroke."

"Really? Well, I had some good advice on the sixteenth from my caddy," she said, smiling at Razor.

"Could you come to the presentation table, please?" George said.

"Yes. I'll be there in a second." George left, and she turned back at Razor. "Why were you so sure the seven would be a better club selection?"

"I'm just good with distances," he told her.

"Targets?"

"Maybe." His face never changed as he answered.

She leaned close and said quietly, "You're an operator. A SEAL."

He took a sip of his beer and didn't respond.

"That's OK. I get it. Thank you for your service. Will you wait for me? Don't leave, please. I'll buy you another beer."

"Uh, sure. OK." Razor was a bit confused. Why would someone like her want to buy someone like him a beer? He sighed. It would be rude to leave now. As she stood to leave so did Razor. He caught himself staring at her legs again as she walked away and he sat back down. His eyes traveled up those long legs to her ass. Hoping no one saw him checking her out, he broke eye contact and adjusted his hat.

Eve walked to the presentation table they had set up. Over the microphone, Razor heard George announce the new awards and the names of the winners and their scores. He clapped along with the others. A few minutes later, she came back with another trophy, shaped like a cup, and set it next to her second place trophy of a golfer taking a swing.

She sat down, and he finally had to ask her what he'd been wondering. "Why are you talking to me?"

"What do you mean?"

"You wear Ralph Lauren. I wear . . . not Ralph Lauren." He looked at his polo shirt.

"You're wearing Izod, and I'm sure your Navy Exchange carries some Ralph Lauren. But so what? I shop at Walmart, Old Navy, and Under Armour too."

Sarcastically, he said, "Yeah, right."

"I'd like to buy you another beer. Yes or no?"

What was the deal with this woman? he thought. "Uh, OK." *This is not some woman from the bar. She's different.*

Eve caught a server's attention and ordered a beer for him and another glass of wine for herself. After a few minutes of uncomfortable silence, he said, "What do you do?"

"Real estate. I'm a Realtor. Mostly condos and houses."

He didn't know what else to say. Again, uncomfortable silence. He watched her as she sipped her wine. When she finished it and stood up, he did too.

"I'm getting hungry, so I'm going to go." She reached into her backpack and pulled out a business card holder. She wrote a number on her card and handed it to him. "It was nice meeting you, Razor. Call me if you'd like to have another drink. Or get something to eat." Then she winked at him.

He took the card as she put the backpack on and picked up her trophies. She gave him one last smile and walked toward the exit.

What the hell just happened? She gave me her card. She wants to see me again? What was with that wink? Scoffing, he took his phone out and called the number she'd written on the card. *Probably a fake number.*

"Hello?" she said.

He almost hung up before she answered. He cleared his throat and said, "Uh, I didn't think this was a real number." Then he added, "Oh, this is Razor."

"Do you get many girls' phone numbers that aren't real, Razor?"

"Not really. No." Still surprised that she had answered the phone, he'd forgotten why he called.

"Hello? Razor?"

"Uh, yeah. I . . . would you like to go out for a burger or something? You said you were hungry."

"Yes. I'd love a burger. I'm outside the doors to the clubhouse," she said.

CHAPTER 2

Razor paid his bill and exited the clubhouse. Outside, he saw Eve talking to another man. *She knows a lot of guys. What does that mean? She must be a member here. She said she was a Realtor, so she probably knows a lot of people. She sure is pretty. Long legs.* Razor stood a few feet away, waiting. He felt like her bodyguard as he looked around, not wanting to interrupt her conversation. *Look at her. She's classy. You're a sasquatch. Just go home.*

"Great job today, Eve. I'll bet you could have been a professional," Fred, the club pro, said.

"Thanks, Fred. Would you believe I once considered it?" she said as Razor began to walk away.

"You'll have to tell me about that another time. Congratulations again and thanks for your donation too," he said.

"Always ready to help out a good cause. I have a niece who has autism." They were raising money for a local school that taught children with autism and other special needs. The school needed some supplies and specialized playground equipment, like swings for wheelchairs. Eve was happy to help because it was personal for her. "Would you excuse me, Fred?" she said, walking quickly to catch up to Razor. "Hey, Razor. Wait up." She stepped in front of him. "Were you ditching me? I thought we were going to grab a burger?"

He stared down at her. "You were being polite. It's OK." He started to take a step to the side, but she stepped with him, blocking him again. Razor was a bit surprised at her unexpected move.

"I don't give my personal number to everyone, and I'd like to talk to you some more. So do you know where we can get a good burger and a beer?"

He hesitated and finally said, "Yes." Razor considered taking her to the Rally Point. It was the bar where his fellow operators hung out, and he loved their burgers. But bringing her there meant she'd see the guys, and he didn't think it was her kind of place.

Eve saw his eyebrows become almost one as he wrinkled his face. "Don't do that."

"Do what?" he asked.

"You have a place in mind, but you don't want to take me because your friends are there. It's OK. I can handle it."

"No. It's not your kind—"

She cut him off. "Razor. What's the name of the place?"

"The Rally Point."

She smiled. "I know it. My dad used to go there sometimes."

"Your dad?" His face softened, although it was difficult to tell through all his facial hair.

"He was a master diver and master chief petty officer."

"That's how you knew," he said, referring to her guess about him being a SEAL.

"I knew because of the way you carried yourself, your hat, and your tattoo. There are a lot of veterans in the area. Come on, let's go there."

"No," he told her.

"Yes."

"No." He crossed his arms defensively.

"*Yes!* Fall out, Razor!" she ordered him. Staring up at this mountain of a man, she crossed her arms and maintained her ground. It was a standoff. All that was missing were their six-shooters and maybe one more person. Who would blink first?

She has pretty eyes, he thought. He kind of liked the way she stood up to him. If she were a man he'd growl and stare. It usually worked, but she wasn't going to be intimidated. He sighed and dropped his arms. "Fine, but I want a mulligan if you don't like it."

"Fair enough." She chuckled. "I'll meet you there." She went to get her golf bag among the line of others in the row nearby but Razor took the bag from her. She strolled to her SUV and opened the back, setting down her trophies and backpack. Razor carefully placed her clubs inside. "See you there."

"Yeah." He couldn't take his eyes off hers. Those green orbs were captivating, and he tried to figure out what they reminded him of. "My woobie," he said before she turned away.

"Excuse me?"

"Your eyes. They remind me of one of the green colors on my woobie."

"Your woobie." She repeated the word with a slight inflection.

"My poncho liner. It's attached to the poncho."

"Believe it or not, I know what a woobie is. I've just never had my eyes compared to one before," she said.

"It was a compliment." Razor wanted to make sure she wasn't offended.

"Thank you. Meet you at the Rally Point." She turned and headed for the driver's side. Razor followed and held her door, which surprised her. He closed it, then watched as she drove off.

"That figures. A BMW. I'm never going to hear the end of it," he mumbled as he walked to his Ford truck and drove to the Rally Point. Along the way he thought about what he'd said. *Stupid. Comparing her eyes to a woobie. What a stupid thing to say,* he thought. What should he have said? *Emeralds or something. That's what guys say. They compare her eyes to emeralds. That's a green stone, right?* He sighed and shook his head.

*****

As Eve drove to the bar, she thought about the last man she had dated and the one before that. They both wore suits to their jobs. One was a loan officer at a bank. The other had a PhD and was a professor at the local university. They were nice and treated her to dinners at expensive restaurants. There was nothing wrong with them, but Eve had ended the relationships after a few dates. There was even an officer from the navy base who'd asked her out, but she'd declined. She wasn't sure what she was looking for in a man, but they weren't it. Eve didn't need the house in the suburbs with a white picket fence, two children, and the husband coming home to dinner waiting on the table. Far from it. That was not Eve.

Eve was a strong, independent woman who had graduated college, become a Realtor, and opened her own business. A business she'd worked hard to make successful. She didn't need a man to take care of her. She wanted an equal partner. Someone who respected her and her work ethic.

Eve also wanted some passion. Maybe she hadn't given those relationships enough time. Was passion something that developed gradually? Or would it happen immediately?

This man, Razor, was not the type who typically asked her out. Had she been too forward? Too aggressive? Under normal circumstances, their paths would likely not have crossed unless he needed to buy a house or condo. If he hadn't made the club recommendation and subsequent explanation, she probably would have thanked him and let it go at that. But she was curious. She wanted to know more about him. He'd given up his day to volunteer at a charity event. Was he told to do it, or was it for some other reason?

*****

As Razor pulled into the parking lot, he realized how he was dressed. The guys would have a field day with that as well. Eve parked next to him, and when she opened her door, he said, "I'll take you anywhere else. Please."

"No. Come on, big guy. Trust me. It's going to be fine."

"The guys aren't . . . I usually don't dress like this."

"You look nice. You were at a country club, and it was necessary. They wouldn't have let you wear jeans and a T-shirt. Relax. It'll be fine." She walked to the entrance and waited for him. Razor jogged over and opened the door for her, then followed her inside.

The Rally Point was just as she remembered. Her father had taken her there a few times. She recalled that he brought her when she turned eighteen. Even though she wasn't of legal drinking age, he gave her a beer and said, "I know women aren't supposed to be in combat, but you're old enough to go off to war and fire a weapon, Eve. In some countries you can legally drink. You will have your first drink with your old man before you leave for college. We'll come back on your twenty-first birthday, and you can buy me one." Her mother wasn't pleased, but he'd done the same thing with her older brother. Her father treated his children equally. It's what made Eve who she was and she bought her father that drink on her twenty-first birthday.

The bar was decorated in a typical military motif, mostly navy. Camouflage netting hung from the ceiling in some places. Flags from each service branch adorned the ceiling as well. Under the top of the bar were unit and rank patches from all branches of service. Some of the barstools sported military-themed stickers. A large display of challenge coins was in a rack behind the bar. In one corner stood a sizable mounted anchor with a plaque. On one wall was a shelf lined with model ships. There were wooden tables and chairs in the main area and a pool table and dartboard in another. It had barely changed since Eve had had that drink with her father.

Razor knew everyone in the bar, including the staff. It was known as a navy hangout, especially for the SEAL teams stationed in the area of Little Creek, Virginia. Razor and his team members spent a lot of time at the Rally Point, which was why he was hesitant about taking Eve there now.

Eve walked straight to the bar and said, "Two of Razor's usual beers." She sat on a stool as he joined her. Then, when she knew everyone was watching, she turned to Razor and placed her hand behind his neck, pulling him close. She gently brushed her lips against his.

"No way. Is that Razor?" Guppy asked, glancing over from the pool table. He was one of the younger members on Razor's team and looked up to him as a mentor.

"Who is that chick with him?" Nugget asked. Another team member, Nugget earned his nickname by eating one hundred chicken nuggets on a drunken dare. Razor gave him the nickname.

"That is a woman, not a chick," Tigger said. "Wow, she is hot." Tigger was married and talked a good game, but that's all he did. He was the one team member who always left the bar early to go home to his wife.

*****

Eve let her lips linger close to Razor's as she slowly stopped the kiss. She wasn't sure why she did it. To get it out of the way. To make a statement in front of his friends. Just to see what he'd do. Maybe she didn't have a reason. It wasn't planned. But she felt something different in this kiss. A warmth came over her. It was unlike anything she'd ever experienced. She cautiously removed her hand from his neck, but they remained close, their lips just inches apart. "I don't think you have to worry now."

Razor swallowed. He was at a loss for words. Razor always had a lot in his head and could speak more if he wanted. He just didn't. Now his mind was flooded with even more thoughts about her. "Huh?" he finally managed to grunt.

"They'll be talking more about the kiss than about the way you're dressed," she whispered.

His eyes were drawn back to hers. He noted a small imperfection in the white of her left eye. A very small dark spot. He hadn't noticed it before. *The kiss. That was some kiss.* It not only surprised him but also made him forget everything he'd been concerned about.

The bartender brought their beers and said, "On your tab, Razor?" Razor was still looking at Eve and didn't hear the man. He didn't hear anything. Not the music, not the crack of the pool balls hitting one another—nothing but his beating heart. His mouth suddenly went dry, and his stomach was doing flips.

Eve answered. "No. I got this round and a round for the house. Also, two burgers for Razor and me. Whatever he likes." She pulled a card and her driver's license from her wallet and showed it to the bartender. She said something else, but Razor couldn't hear it.

Then Razor saw the look on the bartender's face. It was respect. "Yes, ma'am. Thank you," the bartender said.

"It won't work," Razor said. His world had come back into focus and he could hear the sounds around him again.

"What won't work?"

"Now they'll give me a hard time about my clothes and the kiss," he said quietly.

"Probably. I tried." She smiled. "I'll be back."

He stood as she did and watched as she walked to the ladies' room. Sitting back down on the stool, he took off his ball cap and ran a hand through his short dark hair. Replacing his hat, he took a sip of his beer.

"Razor, who the hell is that?" asked Tim from logistics support. Another navy man, he worked with the SEAL teams to ensure they had what they needed logistically. Proper, functioning equipment was important for the teams, and Tim helped get their job done.

Razor just stared at him and growled. Tim walked away. "Wayne, what did she show you?" Razor asked the bartender.

"Special VIP card we rarely give out. You get free drinks and a meal. Her dad gave the card to her. You get on that wall, you get the card," Wayne said, nodding toward one of the walls with a few photos on it. He reached for the rope and rang the bell. "A round on Chief Patterson!"

"Hoorah!" everyone yelled.

"What?" Razor wanted to know more about the card and Eve's father.

"Her dad was a navy diver."

"Master chief, yeah."

"They were training. Two SEALs had a problem out in the ocean. He saved their lives and nearly lost his. Patterson. Over there." Wayne pointed to the walls of photos, one of which was dedicated to the SEALs and support personnel who lost their lives in the line of duty. There was another wall of navy personnel attached to SEAL units who did extraordinary things, such as earn the Navy and Marine Corps Medal. That's where the photo was.

Razor leisurely walked to the wall and studied the photo with the man's name on it. Master Chief Roy Patterson. When Eve returned from the restroom, she saw him looking at the photo and joined him.

She smiled proudly. "That's my father."

"Saved some operators?"

"Yes. It was just before he retired. He could have sent some younger guys, but he told them it was too dangerous. They didn't want him to go, but he said he couldn't leave them without trying. I still don't know the exact details, and he doesn't talk about it. All I know is what's written on his citation. I think he still gets Christmas cards from their wives."

"Hmm. Eve Patterson."

"And Razor . . . ?"

"Senior Chief Petty Officer Reston," Razor told her.

"Seriously? You still aren't telling me your first name?" Eve turned her head and looked up at him.

"Razor, are you going to introduce your friend?" Guppy asked.

Razor gave him a look and growled, hoping he'd go away.

But Guppy was persistent and stared back. "OK. Moving on. Nice pants, dude. Been golfing?"

"Yes," Eve said. "I'm Eve Patterson. Razor was my caddy at a charity golf tournament. With his advice for a club change, my team took second place."

"They call me Guppy." He extended his hand, and she gave it a firm shake. "Razor knows golf?"

"Razor! Burgers are up," Wayne called to him.

Thankful for the distraction, Razor placed a hand gently on Eve's back and escorted her to the bar, where they sat down. Eve took a bite of the burger, and when she set it on her plate, Razor looked at her.

"Wow. That is really good. Well done, Razor."

He cracked a small smile and took a bite of his burger.

The guys watched Razor from the pool table. "Is he on a date?" Tigger asked.

Guppy picked up his pool cue and said, "Razor doesn't date. I mean, I've seen him leave with girls from here, but does he date? I don't know."

"Hey, who was that guy in the photo they were looking at?" Nugget asked.

"Chief Roy Patterson," Guppy answered. "Her name is Eve Patterson, so I guess she's a relative."

"What did he do to get on that wall?" Tigger asked.

"I don't know. Before our time," Guppy told them, lining up his stick to take his shot.

Teflon, their boss and team leader, walked in and looked over at Razor and Eve, who were noticeable in their golf gear. Everyone else was in T-shirts or tactical shirts and jeans or tactical pants. Eve's pink polo stood out like a sore thumb. "Is that Razor?"

"Yeah," Nugget said.

"Right. He was volunteering at a charity event. Some golf tournament," Teflon said.

"Oh, that's why he's dressed like that," Nugget said.

"Is that . . . ? No, it can't be," Teflon said, trying to get a better look at Eve.

"What? You know that girl?"

"I don't know. I'm not sure." He walked to the bar and stood next to Razor. "Razor."

"Boss," Razor said, looking at him and standing. Outranking the other men, Razor could dismiss them with a look or a growl. Teflon, however, was the senior enlisted man on their team. A master chief petty officer. Razor gave him the respect he deserved.

"How was the fundraiser?" Teflon asked.

"Good." Razor seemed to forget his manners and didn't say anything else.

Awkward silence once again. Eve set her burger down and took a sip of her beer. "Hello. I'm Eve Patterson. Razor was my caddy today and did a great job. We raised a lot of money for the school and the kids. Razor, you'll have to come to the opening of their new playground when it's finished."

"Nice to meet you. Patterson? As in Chief Patterson?" Teflon asked.

"Yes. He's my father."

Teflon's face changed, and Razor and Eve noticed.

"Is there a problem, Boss?" Razor asked.

"Um, no." He looked at Eve.

Eve smiled, realizing he was one of the two men her dad saved. "Which one are you?"

"Tefflack. They call me Teflon," he said, shaking her hand.

"Nice to see you again. You were at my father's ceremony."

"Yes. I think my mother, and maybe my ex-wife, still send your father Christmas cards."

Eve and Razor exchanged a look. "Told you," she said.

"How is your father?"

"Retired and bored."

"Boss? Her dad . . . you were one of the guys he saved?" Razor asked.

"Yeah. We were in bad shape and didn't have a chance in hell. It was FUBAR—fucked up beyond all recognition. Then this diver came down, and . . . well, I wouldn't be here if her dad didn't do what he did." Teflon thought back to that mission and took a deep breath. He'd had some close calls since then, but to be stuck underwater, running out of air, was not the way he wanted to die. He'd rather take a bullet. "Tell your dad to come down sometime. It'd be good to see him."

"I will," Eve said.

"Well, it was good to see you again." He walked over to the other guys.

"Do you know that chick, Boss?" Guppy asked.

"Hey, give her some respect. I know her father. He saved my life," Teflon said.

"Sorry, Boss."

*****

Kimberly A. Biggerstaff © 2025

Razor looked at Eve. "So Teflon was one of the guys."

"Yeah, seems so." She took the last bite of her burger and grabbed a couple of french fries. "It was a while ago."

"Cool," Razor said.

Eve laughed at him. "Cool? That's what you have to say?"

"Um."

Eve placed a hand on his. "I'm teasing. Want to play pool?"

No. I want you to leave your hand on mine and kiss me again, he thought. "Yeah, sure."

At the pool table, Razor looked at Guppy and said, "We have the next game."

"You can have it now," Guppy said, smiling at him and laying the cue stick on the table.

Razor watched as Eve chose a stick from the rack against the wall. She placed it on the table and rolled it to make sure it was straight. Satisfied, she picked up some chalk and ran it on the tip of the stick.

Catching him staring at her, Eve said, "Something wrong?"

"What? No. You can break," Razor said.

They both reached for the cue ball, and their hands touched. Razor felt something he'd never experienced before, not with any other woman. It was like that adrenaline high he felt after a mission that went well. He pulled his hand away quickly and swallowed the lump in his throat.

"No, we'll shoot for it," Eve said quietly, also feeling a spark. She smiled, taking the cue ball and setting it at one end of the table. Razor cleared the other balls, placing them in their proper spots within the triangle and moving it to the side. Eve lined up the ball and cue stick and hit the cue ball. She watched as it ran the length of the table, hit the bumper at the other end, and came to a rest about four inches from the rail in front of her.

"Nice," Razor said. He took a ball from the triangle and stepped next to her. He repeated the process, but his ball stopped six inches from the rail. "You break."

Eve waited as Razor set up the balls and removed the triangle. She broke and sank a solid ball.

"Hey, I've got ten on Patterson," Guppy said to Nugget.

"You're on," Nugget replied, digging out a ten-dollar bill from his pocket.

Tigger came over to watch the game, along with a few others. More bets were placed among the spectators. Razor gave Tigger his death stare and growled at him when he caught him looking at Eve's ass as she lined up a shot in front of him.

Eve kept sinking her balls. As she lined up her next shot, Razor looked at her. She glanced up, and her green eyes met his brown ones. She smiled and hit the cue ball, again sinking her shot. With two balls left, she missed her next shot, giving Razor his chance.

He sank four balls, then missed. Eve walked in front of Razor to set up her shot. She passed him slowly, having to turn in order to get by him. Her free hand brushed his leg, and she said, "Excuse me." Again, Razor swallowed the lump in his throat and backed up a bit. Even that slight touch made him shiver. She called her shot on the eight ball and sank it to win the game.

Guppy hollered and collected his money, along with the others who'd placed friendly bets.

"Good game." Razor held out his hand to shake in a sign of sportsmanship.

"Thank you. I hope you didn't go easy on me," Eve said, taking his hand and flashing a bright smile as she looked up at him. Their eyes were fixed on each other's as they held hands longer than necessary.

What is this woman doing to me? Razor wondered. Her hand was so soft. *I'll bet all of her skin is soft. She probably uses fancy soaps and has a whole routine.* Eve's handshake was firm. Not one of those weak ones some women gave. He remembered one young woman's handshake that felt like a limp fish. At the time, he wondered if she expected him to kiss the back of her hand. She was the daughter of a rich politician he met at another charity event he'd attended. Razor ran his thumb back and forth over Eve's hand, and the corner of his lip moved upward in a slight smile. Lost in those smoldering eyes again, he didn't even realize he was moving his thumb.

Nugget hit Razor in the arm. "You owe me a beer, Razor. I had my money on you." Razor and Eve broke eye contact and dropped their hands.

"Yeah, OK," Razor said, not paying attention.

Nugget shrugged and went to get a beer on Razor's tab. "Yeehaw. Free beer," Nugget said.

Eve said, "This has been fun. Thank you." She paused. "I'm going to go."

"Oh. Uh, are you sure?" Razor didn't want the night to end. He was enjoying her company and wanted her to stay even if the guys gave him a hard time. She was worth it.

"Yes. It's been a long day. Walk me to my car?"

He put the pool cue down and followed her outside.

"Thank you, Razor. I had a great time," Eve said.

"Me too." He took her hand and held it. He leaned in for a kiss but stopped when an operator from another team walked by.

"Hey, Razor." The youngster nodded at them.

"Hey." He pulled back and stood tall. Suddenly nervous, he put his hands in his pockets and asked, "Are you OK to drive home?"

"Yes."

"So may I call you?" he asked her.

"I hope you do." She smiled at him.

Her teeth are so white and perfect. She has a beautiful smile. Again, his stomach did flips, and he felt a tingle through his body.

"You're staring," she whispered.

"Sorry. You have a beautiful smile," he managed to say. He opened her door for her, and she got in.

Disappointed he didn't kiss her, she said, "Thanks again, Razor."

"Zack," he said out of the blue. Normally, he wouldn't have told her his name so soon. As a matter of fact, he couldn't remember the last time he'd told a woman his first name. But he felt something special about her. This woman was getting to him. He definitely would call her.

"Zack." She smiled as she said his name. "Give me a call, Zack." She drove off as he watched. Then, when he couldn't see her taillights anymore, he went back inside the bar. The guys gave him hell.

*****

Eve smiled as she drove away. She glanced in the rearview mirror and saw him standing there. She could still feel his thumb gently moving along her hand when they shook hands after the pool game. When she had looked into his dark eyes, she had seen so many things. Confidence, for sure. But there was sorrow as well. She'd seen it once before in her father's eyes after he returned from a deployment. A sailor had been lost. Eve had been young then and didn't know the details of the sailor's death, but she knew her father felt the loss of this young man deep in his heart.

She wondered what had happened to leave that mark in Razor's eyes. Would it fade in time, or would it always be there? Eve wanted to know so much more about him.

*****

The next day Razor changed his mind. Eve Patterson was not for him. She was aggressive. She made the first move by manipulating him into asking her out. Then she kissed him in the bar. *What kind of woman does that?* Razor finished loading the washer, then sat on the couch. Flipping the channels, he found a cop show he liked. *Hmm. She kind of reminds me of Eve.* Eve. He remembered the way she didn't back down about taking her to the Rally Point. It kind of turned him on. She knew what she wanted and went after it. Maybe he should give her a chance. One date. A real date with none of the guys around. If he didn't like it, no harm done.

It was difficult to wait, but a couple of days later, he called her. "Hi, it's Razor."

"Zack?" She preferred to call him by his real name.

"Uh, yeah. I'd like to take you out tonight. Sorry for the short notice, but we have . . . training coming up, and I may not be able to call you for a while."

"Training, right." She knew that could either really mean training or he was deploying. "Tonight? Yes, I'd love to go out."

Taking charge, he said, "I'll pick you up at six thirty. We'll go to dinner at the Porch on Long Creek. Text me your address."

"OK. I'm looking forward to it. See you at six thirty, Zack." She disconnected the call and texted him her address.

CHAPTER 3

Razor went to the door and rang the bell. He had gotten a haircut and trimmed his beard so that it was a little shorter and neater. He wiped his hands on his slacks, hoping they weren't sweaty. *Maybe this was a mistake.* But when she opened the door and smiled, he pushed that thought away. Every time she smiled at him, he melted.

"May I help you?" She acted as if she didn't know who he was, but the slight lift at the corner of her mouth gave her away. "Oh, hello, Zack. I didn't recognize you without your ball cap."

He smiled back at her. "Uh, yeah." He ran a hand through his dark hair. "Are you ready?"

"Yes. Come in for a second, and I'll grab my purse."

He stepped into her condo but stayed near the door. It was a large open space, and he immediately knew it was expensive. She picked up her purse from the sofa and returned to him.

"You look really nice," he said. She was wearing a blue dress that ended just above her knees and low heels.

"Thank you. You clean up good too. I like the shirt."

"Thanks." He was wearing slacks and a button-down shirt with his cowboy boots that he'd spent an hour shining. He made a special trip to the mall and found a Calvin Klein shirt on sale. Razor liked the color and the vertical stripes. He would have shelled out full price for it but got lucky. Following her down the stairs to his truck, he tried not to stare at her legs. He was a leg man and enjoyed looking at hers. His thoughts drifted as he imagined running his hands up her legs and he smiled slightly. He unlocked his truck and opened the door, glad he had washed it and had the inside detailed. It was only three years old, and he took care of it, but he wanted it to be perfect for her. Everything should be perfect. Again his eyes drifted to her legs as she stepped on the running board and climbed inside.

"Have you been to the Porch before?" he asked when he got in.

"No."

"Really? Good."

He drove up US-60 along the coast and through the state park to West Great Neck Road, then turned again where all the boats were docked. As he pulled into the parking lot, she said, "I've never been here, but I sold a home on Buccaneer Road and one on Adam Keeling Road." She pointed in the general direction of both houses.

"Nice homes."

Turning off the truck, he came around, opened her door, and helped her down. Razor wanted to hold her hand but instead placed his hands in his pockets as they walked to the restaurant. It was on the Lynnhaven River and had seating outside; you could even arrive by boat. They sat inside.

"What about you? Have you been here before?" she asked him.

"No, but it was recommended. Supposed to be good."

They engaged in additional small talk, learning more about each other. Razor was comfortable around her and let his guard down a little. She had been a typical navy brat, living on military bases around the world. She told him that it was difficult at times when her father was away on ships or deployed. But she also said she loved the traveling and was lucky to have lived in foreign countries.

"What about you, Zack?" Eve asked, taking a bite of her seared scallops.

"I grew up in Texas. Sort of in the country. About an hour north of Houston. We'd go down to Galveston sometimes. The beach."

"What made you join the navy?"

He smiled and said, "A recruiter."

Laughing at his humor, Eve replied, "Can I get a little more?" She was trying to get the normally reserved man to open up. Eve felt there was more to him behind his gruff facade.

"I played football in high school."

"Defense?"

He smiled. "Yeah. I went to Texas A&M for a year, played ball there. I kept eyeing the Corps of Cadets. Their sense of pride and camaraderie. Dad was navy for a few years. Said the food was good. Spoke to a recruiter. Got a SEAL challenge contract before I enlisted."

"So you joined the navy because your dad said the food was good?"

He laughed. "Yeah, but Dad never ate at an air force base. It's a totally different experience." He set his fork down after finishing his catch of the day and sipped his beer.

"I was kidding. Sounds like you were looking for something more, and you're patriotic."

"I guess."

After Eve refused dessert, Razor paid the bill and asked what she wanted to do. "You don't have anything planned?" Eve asked him. She'd be surprised if he hadn't had something to follow up dinner.

"I do."

"Lead the way, Senior Chief," she teased him.

*****

Eve was surprised when they arrived at the Apex Entertainment complex. He purchased two fun passes, and they went on their way. They played some games and bowled, and then they came to a designated area with a sign that read AXE THROWING.

"You can't be serious . . . are you?" she asked.

Razor smiled, and they went to the check-in desk to sign safety waivers and collect their equipment. "Heels aren't appropriate, ma'am. Do you have other shoes?" the man told her.

"Oh. Well, no," she said, looking down at her feet.

"Wait here." Razor returned a minute later with socks and tennis shoes. "I keep a go bag in my truck. They're clean," he said, handing her the socks.

She raised her eyebrows. "Uh, a little big, though," she said, looking at his shoes.

"We can do something else if you want." He seemed disappointed.

"No." She took them, and holding on to him with one hand, she slipped the socks and shoes on.

The man at the counter looked at her disapprovingly, eyeing the shoes that were huge on her. They looked like clown shoes on her feet. Razor growled at him when it seemed like he was going to say something. "Signed a waiver. Appropriate footwear," Razor said.

"OK," the man said simply.

*****

Razor took the axes, and they walked to their assigned lane, which was about five feet wide and twelve feet deep. A three-foot wooden barrier separated them from the next lane, with the fencing on top of the barrier continuing to the ceiling. Basically, it was a wooden and fenced cage. The wall at the end of the lane was wooden with a black spot surrounded by a red ring and then a blue one creating the target. It was worn with axe marks that had chipped away pieces of the wood.

"You're going to have to show me how to do this," Eve told him.

"Does that mean I have a chance at winning?" he asked, teasing her. Razor took an axe and stepped to a line on the floor. "It's a little like darts, but you throw an axe. You can throw two-handed or one-handed." Razor held the axe with two hands, placed it over his head, and threw it. It landed just above the bull's-eye.

"Nice throw."

"One-handed, elbow in, straight, and . . ." He threw another axe and hit the bull's-eye.

"What do you recommend?" Eve asked him.

"Two-handed first." He gave her an axe. "It's made for throwing, so it's not as heavy as a hatchet. Hold it like a golf club. Thumbs on top. Light grip."

Eve felt the weight of the axe and held it like a golf club but without wrapping her pinkie and first finger. Razor was standing next to her and showed her the motion over his head. Eve started to raise the axe, then hesitated.

"You OK?"

"Yeah."

Sensing her uncertainty, he took the axe and set it on the table. Then he stood behind her and placed his hands on hers. "Stagger your stance. Pretend you're holding the axe. Let's get the motion. Nice and slow." She let his hands guide hers up and then down. Eve inhaled as she felt his body close to hers as they rocked back. The aroma of his cologne tickled her senses, and the slight tobacco smell took her back to the days when her father occasionally smoked a cigar on their back porch. They repeated the throwing motion twice more.

She felt comfortable in his arms, and he enjoyed holding her. "OK," he said. As he looked down at her, he thought about kissing her on the cheek but didn't. Then he let her go and handed her an axe.

Eve took it, and remembering what he said, she raised it, rocked back a little, and threw it. Bull's-eye. "Whoo-hoo!" Eve yelled.

Razor stared at the target as Eve hugged him excitedly. He couldn't help but smile as he looked down at her in his arms. Gazing into her green eyes, he kissed her on the lips without thinking about it.

When they parted, she said, "Let's go again."

*****

Razor took his shoes back from her, and Eve held his arm as she put her heels on. They returned the axes, and he took her hand as they walked back to his truck.

"That was great! We'll have to come back when I'm dressed more appropriately," Eve told him. "Let's go to the Rally Point."

He noticed how excited she still was after spending an hour throwing axes. "Are you sure? Aren't your arms sore?"

"No. They might be tomorrow, but let's go to the bar." When they arrived at his truck, she turned to him. Letting go of his hand, she placed hers on his arm and searched his eyes. "How long are you going to be . . . training?"

"I don't know."

"Well, let's stop in for a drink or two. My treat," she offered.

"No. I pay on this date." Razor was brought up to be polite and a gentleman. He opened doors and held them, and he always stood up when a woman approached a table. *Yes, sir* and *no, ma'am* were a part of his vocabulary long before he joined the navy. And he paid when he asked a girl out. He let Eve get away with using her VIP card at the Rally Point, even though he'd asked her out for the meal. He'd left the tip to make himself feel better. He wouldn't call himself old-fashioned; it was just the way he was raised.

Eve smiled and took his hand. "OK."

As he held the door of his truck, Razor stepped closer and placed his hand on her cheek. He closed the distance, letting go of the door and leaning in to kiss her. He pressed his lips against hers gently. Then he pressed just a little harder. Their lips parted, and they began exploring. Razor could smell her perfume as he moved a hand to the small of her back. The fragrance reminded him of taking pictures in a bluebonnet field when he was a boy. Slowly, he pulled away from her. Her chest heaving, she said breathlessly, "You might have to take me to the hospital."

"What's wrong?" he asked, thinking she might have pulled a muscle throwing an axe.

"I think I have butterflies in my stomach."

He laughed and gave her a quick kiss. As they drove, Razor took her hand in his. They glanced at each other and smiled. They didn't talk much on the way to the bar, but they held hands the entire time. Occasionally, Razor moved his thumb along her hand, gently caressing it. When they arrived, he didn't let go of her hand. Staying in the truck, he turned to her. With his left hand, he brushed her hair back as they slowly closed the gap between them and their lips met.

*****

As they kissed, Razor had his hand on Eve's thigh as she leaned over the truck's console. He was slowly inching his way up her smooth skin, his thumb within striking distance of his target. He was about to slip it under her lace lingerie when she said, "Zack?"

"Hmm?"

"I'd rather not do this here."

They pulled away and laughed. Razor tucked his shirt back into his pants, and Eve pulled her dress down and slipped her heels back on.

"Making out in a truck is not like it was when I was sixteen," Razor commented. "My old truck had a bench seat." He grinned.

It was Eve's turn to smile. "There's more room in the back seat. No console to get in the way." Razor had a Ford F-150 SuperCrew, and the back seat was spacious.

He laughed. "I thought you didn't want to do it here?"

"Yeah. Maybe we should go inside and cool off."

"I agree."

When Razor and Eve walked in, the guys once again gave Razor a hard time about the way he was dressed. The catcalls were all for Razor. He expected it and didn't say anything. Eve walked to the table where Guppy, Nugget, and Tigger were sitting. Razor growled and stared at them like he had many times before. They understood his silent order, and they all stood up.

"Take my seat, ma'am," Nugget said, pulling out his chair.

"Thank you . . . ," Eve said as she tried to recall his name.

"Nugget," he supplied.

Eve looked at them and said, "Guppy, Nugget, and . . ."

"Tigger," Tigger said as they waited for Razor to sit so that they knew it was OK to retake their own seats.

"Nugget, how did you get that name?" Eve asked.

"Someone bet me I couldn't eat one hundred chicken nuggets. I did." He smiled proudly. "Razor started calling me Nugget."

"I'm impressed," Eve said.

"Don't be. They were tiny," Guppy said.

"No, they weren't."

"Guppy? How about you? I hope you didn't eat a bunch of goldfish," Eve said as she smiled at him.

They laughed. "No, ma'am. Uh, we were crossing a river, and somehow a few fish got into my uniform."

"Once we were clear, he dropped his drawers, and all these fish started pouring out." Tigger laughed, and Nugget placed his hands together to imitate a fish swimming.

"Kid thought they were piranha and about sh—" Razor got caught up in the story and almost cussed. He didn't want to do that in front of Eve. She was a lady, and he didn't talk that way in front of ladies. "Well, he, uh . . . almost got rid of an MRE and not in a nice way."

"You can say it," Guppy said. "I almost crapped myself." If he'd been telling the story to a guy, he would have said the word *shit*.

"Lady is present." Razor narrowed his eyes at Guppy.

"Thank you, but it's OK. I'm the daughter of an enlisted navy man, and I have a brother." Eve appreciated Razor's politeness. "Who gave you that nickname? Why not Fish?"

The men were quiet. It was as if she broached a taboo subject. "Uh, they had a guy called Fish once. He got another assignment. Cobra named me," Guppy said quietly. Silently, they raised their bottles and drank.

Realizing he must have been a fallen comrade, Eve changed the subject. "Teflon isn't around?"

"No, ma'am. He's preparing for our training," Guppy told her.

Razor finally sat down next to Eve, and the others pulled up two more chairs from another table. "What would you like to drink?" Razor asked Eve.

"Beer, Razor, if you're buying," Tigger said.

Razor glared at him. "Not buying for you."

"Red wine, please," Eve said, and he went to get the drinks.

"I guess I should get going anyway. The wife is waiting," Tigger said.

"You're married?" Eve asked.

"Yes, ma'am, and I got a little girl on the way," he said proudly, pulling the ultrasound picture from his wallet.

"Here we go," Guppy said with a sigh.

Tigger showed Eve the photo. "That's sweet."

"Let's hope she looks like his wife," Nugget said.

"Don't make her go into early labor," Guppy said, laughing.

"What?" Tigger asked.

"Sex can induce labor," Guppy told him.

"It can? How do you know?" Tigger wasn't sure he believed him.

"My sister. The last month of her pregnancy, she was so big, she was begging her husband for sex to get it out of her."

Eve looked at Tigger, who seemed concerned. "I wouldn't worry about it. The baby will come when she's ready."

"I'll see you," Tigger said. "See you tomorrow, Razor," he said as Razor returned with their drinks.

"Later." He gave Eve her wine and sat back down with his beer.

After a few minutes, Eve whispered to Razor that she was going to the ladies' room. When she stood, so did he. Guppy and Nugget stood as well.

A group of four men walked in and went to the bar. "The Rally Point!" one of them yelled. They had been barhopping and were already feeling good.

"Four shots, barman," the same man said. "Hey, Leo, do I smell squid?"

"Yeah, I think you're right, Pete," Leo said.

Guppy and Nugget looked at them, but Razor kept the youngsters in check. "Easy, boys." As the oldest and ranking member of the three of them, Razor knew it was his job to make sure they stayed out of trouble. Guppy and Nugget were young, and sometimes their emotions got the better of them.

The four men at the bar downed their shots and ordered beers. There were other SEALs and navy personnel in the bar, but the foursome didn't care and kept making derogatory comments about the navy and praising the army.

The bar was a square, and the men were standing at the side closest to the restrooms. Pete was leaning against the bar when he saw Eve and blocked her path. "Hey, honey. How about welcoming a soldier back home?"

"No, thanks." She tried to step around him, but he wouldn't let her by.

"Come on. You're looking hot in that dress. Let's go somewhere, and I'll take it off." He grinned at her, and his buddies laughed and watched.

"I said no."

Razor rose from his chair when he saw the interaction. Guppy and Nugget stood too, ready to back the big man up. He didn't need it, but it was what teammates did.

Razor looked at Eve, who made eye contact and shook her head slightly.

"Hey, baby. Let me show you my artillery." Pete laughed again, and his buddies did too. Others nearby took offense as they watched them. The ones who knew Eve was with Razor looked over at him. He was standing his ground. If he gave the word, all hell would break loose.

Eve glared at Pete and said strongly, "For the last time, I'm telling you no."

Then Pete made his mistake. He reached his hand around her waist to pull her in for a kiss. Before Razor could move, Eve stepped back and kneed Pete in the groin. With her right arm, she reached under his right arm, grabbing his shoulder and leaning her right hip into his. Then she turned and pulled him over her shoulder, and he fell to the ground with a thud.

"Holy shit!" Guppy yelled.

"I'm in love," Nugget said.

Razor smiled proudly as Eve stepped over Pete and walked to him. She said, "Why don't we go back to my place." It was more of a statement than a question as she grabbed her purse and his hand and pulled him out the door.

*****

Razor walked her to the door of her condo, took her hands, and kissed her good night. It was a sweet, short kiss.

"I had a really nice time, Zack."

"I did too. You know, I normally don't tell anyone my real name," he said, letting her hands go.

Smiling at him, Eve said, "Well, thank you for telling me. Would you like to come in?" She took her keys out of her purse and began to unlock the door.

He looked at his watch. "Um, yes, but training starts at 0500 hours. I still have a few things to do before then." There was nothing he'd like more than to go inside with her and see what happened. He'd love to take her in his arms and make love to her. *I want to feel your lips against mine as I run my hands down your waist, along your thigh, and . . .* He cleared his throat and took a step back. He really did have to double check some things before he reported to base in the morning. He had to tell her it was training for security purposes, but in reality he was flying overseas with his team on a mission. Hopefully, he'd be back soon.

"Oh, that's early. I understand. Thanks again." She opened the door and stepped inside. Turning to him, she called his name as he began to leave. "Zack?"

"Yes."

"Stay safe and call me when you can."

"Yeah, I will." He turned and walked slowly away. To himself he said, "I will definitely call you." He let out a deep breath. Razor wondered why he didn't go inside with her. It was true he had some things to do, but he could have stayed. Would he have stayed if it was some other girl? Probably. He wasn't a manwhore, but he'd had a few one-night stands. It was too soon to sleep with Eve. Not on the first date. The second date might be a different story. He smiled to himself. *I need a cold shower.*

*****

The mission lasted two weeks, and Razor returned on a Tuesday morning. After a mandatory debriefing and stowing his gear, Zack went to his apartment to get cleaned up and to rest. He wasn't able to sleep much on the plane because all he thought about was Eve. He showered and fell asleep in a recliner with the TV on.

He woke up two hours later. As he looked at his watch, once again Eve invaded his mind. The time he'd spent with her was fun and exciting. He was attracted to her, but something was still nagging at him. He'd had time to think about it, and he still felt she was too good for him. She was too classy, and he was sure she made more money than he did. Razor knew it shouldn't matter, but it still bothered him. It didn't help that the guys teased him about her BMW and his Ford. He didn't understand why she was attracted to him.

Even though he had those feelings of doubt, he couldn't stop thinking about her. She'd gotten in his head. He was able to manage it on the mission, but as soon as it was over, she crept back into his thoughts. The axe throwing was fun, and the way she handled herself with that guy at the bar was awesome. He told her that he'd call her when he returned. The one thing he was proud of was that when he said he'd do something, he did it.

*****

The first few days that Razor was gone were fine. Eve was busy with work, showing houses and condos in the area. By the end of the week, while sitting at her desk in her office, she found herself wondering where Razor was and what he was doing. Staring at her computer, she opened a new tab on her browser and typed his name. She found two articles about him being named high school football player of the week and a high school all-American. The last one she read was about him earning a scholarship and committing to Texas A&M to play football.

Eve leaned back in her chair. Did he give up his scholarship to enlist? She remembered that he told her he played for a year, so she didn't think he'd gotten hurt. He said he watched the Corps of Cadets. He was a patriotic man who gave up playing football to serve his country. Impressive.

The next day, Eve was showing a house to a young couple. They had a three-year-old girl and one on the way. The little girl twirled in her princess dress in the middle of the kitchen. Eve smiled at her, and for the first time in her life, she thought about having children. After college, she'd been focused on her career working for a real estate company. She dated, but she didn't want to jump into having a family. Then she decided to start her own company and was so busy that it hadn't crossed her mind.

"Miss Patterson?" The woman interrupted Eve's thoughts.

"Yes, sorry."

"You said they renovated it? When was that?"

"Three years ago," Eve said. *What has this man done to me?* She finished showing the house and drove home, thinking about him the entire way.

*****

"Hello, Eve. It's Razor."

Kimberly A. Biggerstaff © 2025

Eve's face lit up, happy that he had called her. "Hey. Are you back? Did training go well?" she asked.

"Yeah, fine. I just wanted to let you know we're home." He preferred to forget about it. He needed time away, even if it was a day or two.

"I'm at home. Why don't you come over?" Eve said. She really wanted to see him, realizing that she'd missed him.

"What?" Razor called like he said he would, but he didn't expect to see her. Not today. Maybe he should have waited another day or two before calling her.

"Come over to my place. I mean, if you want to."

He wanted nothing more than to see her, but he wasn't sure. Those doubts crept into his mind again. He felt the gauze bandage under his shirt. He was told to rest and take it easy for the next few days, but they didn't tell him where he should do his resting.

When he took too long to answer, Eve spoke. "Zack? Is something wrong? I thought things were fine before you left."

"Yeah, no, things were great. I guess I'm still in training mode. I'm also not used to having someone to phone after," he admitted. "Yes, I'd like to see you. Do you want me to bring anything? Pizza, beer, or wine?"

"Yes, that'll be great," she told him. "Pizza and beer. I have wine."

"Uh, do you mind if I dress casual?"

"Not at all. Wear whatever makes you comfortable."

*****

They ate half the pizza and then went out to her balcony. "This is a great view," Razor told her.

"Yes. It is. You should see the sunrise."

He grinned slightly and looked at the beach below. There was tension in the air. A good kind.

"Come sit with me. I missed talking to you," she said as she sat on a lounge chair. She was barefoot and wore jeans and a long-sleeved seersucker shirt. The cuffs were folded just below her elbow.

He noticed her watch. A gold one. *Probably a Rolex.* He laughed. "I'm not known for my conversations." He saw her shiver. "Are you cold?"

"Maybe a little."

He sat on the end of her chair. "This is a little small for both of us." If he'd had a jacket, he would have given it to her, but he'd left it in the truck.

"Yeah, you're right. Let's go sit on the couch." He followed her inside. Without warning, she turned and hugged him. "I missed you."

He winced a little, but she didn't notice. When she looked up at him, he leaned over and brushed his lips with hers. The kiss reminded him of the ones in his truck in the parking lot of the Rally Point. His stomach started doing that thing it did when he was near her. It flipped and did somersaults. He sat on the couch and pulled her next to him. Gazing into her eyes, he closed the gap. They kissed again, and this time he rested a hand on her leg. He moved his hand to her waist and began to untuck her blouse. She pulled his T-shirt up to touch his skin with her left hand. But it wasn't skin her fingers grazed. It was a gauze bandage.

"Zack? What's this?" She started to take his shirt off to get a better look, but he held her hand, stopping her.

"It's nothing."

"Nothing?" She poked it.

"Grrr!" he growled through gritted teeth.

"It's not nothing." She pulled his shirt up and looked at the bandage. A small red spot was forming. "It's bleeding."

"You poked it."

"Let me see if I have something. Take your shirt off." Eve went to the hall bathroom and pulled out a first aid kit from under the sink. When she returned to the living room, she saw that he was just sitting there. "Zack, take your shirt off." But he didn't move. She sat next to him, then put the first aid kit on the table in front of them. Looking at him, she placed a hand on his leg. She gave him a few moments and then said, "If you'd rather change the bandage yourself, the bathroom is down the hall."

"It's classified," he said quietly, looking down at his lap as he held his left hand over the bandage. He wanted to tell her about what happened but couldn't. Other than his teammates, having someone to talk to and share things with was not something he was used to.

"I figured. I wasn't going to ask. I'm a navy brat, Zack. I know there are things you do, places you go, that you can't talk about. I just want you to know that I'm here for the things you can talk about." She smiled at him.

Razor looked up and saw that smile. He melted. "You have a nice smile." Then he slowly took his shirt off. "It's just a flesh wound."

"For some reason I think you're downplaying it. Are you supposed to be walking around?"

"I wanted to see you." He leaned over and kissed her.

She smiled and then looked at the bandage. "I need to take this off." He moved his right arm and straightened up so that she could get better access to it. As she carefully pulled the bandage from his skin, she couldn't help but glance at his muscular chest and torso. *Wow,* she thought. He was tight and ripped. Six-pack abs, with barely any body fat. She imagined herself resting her head on that chest.

"Eve." He startled her from her thoughts, and she continued pulling the bandage. She cleaned the wound with antiseptic.

"Does that hurt?" she asked gently, dabbing away the blood.

"Not much."

"This is a little more than a flesh wound. You may need to have someone look at these stitches. I'll put a butterfly on it for now." She finished and covered the wound with a clean bandage. "It wasn't bad. The bleeding, I mean. But you should get it checked again."

"You did fine. Thank you," he said. As she cleaned up and threw away the dirty bandage, he took a big gulp of his beer.

"Are you on pain meds?" she asked.

He gestured to his beer. "Just this. May I have another beer?" he asked. "I'm fine."

She brought him another, then reached for her wine. Razor picked up his shirt to put it back on, but she snatched it, tossed it behind her, and kissed him.

He took the wineglass from her hand and set it on the table. "Tell me about this tattoo." She touched his right arm just above the biceps.

"It's Neptune on a sea dragon with his trident."

"Antoine Coysevox?" she asked.

"I guess." He kissed her on the neck.

"Have you seen it?"

Razor was more interested in her neck than talking about a tattoo. "Seen what?"

"The statue." She pushed him away to stop his kissing.

"Yes. I visited the Louvre in Paris once. I liked it. He has a trident. One of our symbols." Her hair was pulled back in a ponytail, and he reached around and gently tugged on the band, removing it so that her hair fell around her shoulders. He kissed her neck again and began undoing the top button on her shirt.

"What about the King Neptune statue at Neptune Park? On the boardwalk at Virginia Beach."

"I've seen it. It's nice. I like Coysevox's version with the dragon."

"It's a horse."

Razor stopped kissing her, feeling the need to give her his interpretation of the statue. "It's a sea dragon or seahorse. He's wrangling it, like a cowboy. Controlling it so he can use it to pull his chariot."

Eve smiled like a Cheshire cat, and Razor asked, "Were you testing me?"

"I think there's more to you than you let on." Eve scratched at his beard. "I'd like to learn more about Zachary Reston."

"I'm just a door-kicker."

"No, you aren't." Eve moved forward to kiss him. She pushed him back on the couch so that he was lying down and then continued kissing him. His beard tickled her face. She felt his hands gently hold her waist and then slowly move under her blouse. The moment his fingertips touched her skin, she experienced something she'd never felt before. This rough-looking man evoked a passion in her, and she wanted more of him. Not only did she want to know more about the man, Zachary Reston, but at this moment, she wanted to feel his body. Wanted to feel his hands as they explored her body.

*****

Razor jerked awake and looked at the luminescent hands on his watch. Three fifteen. Turning his head, he looked at Eve lying next to him. She was on her side, facing away from him. Staring at the ceiling, Razor could barely feel the sheet partially covering him. It was so soft and comfortable. *What did they call it? Thread count.* It had to be expensive. He was a guy, so he didn't know about that stuff. He looked around the bedroom. There was a small amount of light coming from the bathroom. He saw the chair and ottoman in one corner. The dresser was modern but again looked expensive. *What am I doing here? This isn't me. I get my furniture from Walmart or IKEA.* Razor felt out of place.

Carefully sliding out of bed, he noiselessly padded to the bathroom, picking up his clothes from the floor. For a big man, he was surprisingly quiet. Even the bathroom looked expensive. The towels were embroidered with the Harrods brand on them. *That's an expensive store in London.* He'd never been to England but had heard of the store. *That guy Princess Di was seeing when she was killed. His father owned that store.* As quietly as he could, Razor dressed and then opened the door, carrying his boots. The ambient glow from the night-light in the bathroom let him see her in bed. The sheet was under her right arm. Her back was flawless, and he remembered running his hand over her smooth skin and making love to her only hours earlier.

God, she is so hot. What are you doing here, Razor? This woman is better than you. She owns a condo on the beach and wears a Rolex. She probably dates businessmen who make three times what you do. She's beautiful and smart. Never mind. Get out while you can. Like a thief, he stealthily crept to the bedroom door, slid through it, and walked out to the living area. Putting his boots on, he suddenly remembered something. *Damn. The alarm.* He glanced at the balcony. No, that door was armed as well. He stared at the alarm pad. He really didn't want to disarm it, though he could have. Something the navy taught him for his job.

"Zack? What are you doing?" Eve asked, staring at him.

Shit.

He glanced at her but was silent. She was wearing a fluffy robe, and her long brown hair hung on both sides of her shoulders. Even at this early hour, after just waking up, she was beautiful. She waited for an answer, but he didn't know what to say. The silence was becoming unbearable, and finally Eve walked over to the alarm pad. Blocking his view, she punched in the code. Then she moved to the door and opened it. He hesitated for a second and then retreated slowly, like a dog who'd been kicked out for getting in the kitchen garbage. She closed the door behind him, and he heard the dead bolt, the chain, and the lock engage; he was sure she reset the alarm too.

Worst getaway ever. She was the first woman he'd slept with who had an alarm system. He also had never been caught leaving. Suddenly, he felt like a jerk. He moved slowly down the hall toward the stairs. *So this was the walk of shame.* Razor had never felt like this when he'd left a woman's place before. He sat in his truck for a couple of minutes, thinking about what he'd just done. *I snuck out like she was a one-night stand. Idiot. I ruined it. But I always leave. She's too good for me anyway. I'm just a door-kicker.* Starting the truck, he drove back to his apartment. He thought about other times he'd left women in the middle of the night or early morning. It had been more or less understood that they were just having fun. He'd never felt guilty, and there had never been any hard feelings.

He didn't sleep around a lot. In fact, he'd turned down more women than he'd slept with.

But something was different this time, he realized as he pulled into the parking lot of his apartment complex. Inside, he went straight to his bedroom. He stripped down to his briefs, crawled into bed, and stared at the ceiling. "You're an idiot, Razor. Why did you leave?"

*****

Eve leaned against the door after setting the alarm. "Unbelievable," she said, shaking her head. She walked over to the coffee table to pick up his beer bottle and her glass of wine. Taking them to the kitchen, she dumped the contents in the sink and rinsed the wineglass. After placing the glass in the dishwasher, Eve threw his bottle away. She paused, then retrieved a clean glass and the wine. Pouring herself some, she sat at the kitchen table to reflect on what had happened.

She was angry and hurt and also disappointed that he tried to sneak out. *Why would he do that?* Eve thought they'd enjoyed each other's company. She had hoped to wake up in his arms or at the very least next to him. Instead, he slunk away in the middle of the night like it was a one-night stand. He made her feel cheap and that hurt. "Your loss, Senior Chief Reston." She finished the wine and went back to bed.

*****

Waking up at seven, Razor did a weight workout in his spare room. His wound hurt a little, so he didn't go very heavy or hard with the weights. Then he went for a short run outside. After downing a protein shake and eating some breakfast, he showered and dressed. He had the day off and ran some errands, which included restocking his fridge. It was difficult trying not to think about Eve. She kept appearing in his thoughts. Razor couldn't get last night out of his mind. The way her body felt as he trailed his fingertips along it. He was right. Her skin was so soft and slightly tanned. She had a small mole just under her right breast. He caught himself smiling and shook his head. *Forget her. You blew it.*

*****

At about two in the afternoon, he drove to the Rally Point. Guppy and Nugget were playing pool as usual. They were young and single and didn't worry about anyone but themselves. Razor remembered when he was in his mid- to late twenties. Not like it was that long ago. He was only thirty-eight, with a birthday coming up.

"There he is. Hey, Razor! Did you see your girl last night?" Guppy asked.

"Shouldn't you be recuperating?" Nugget asked.

"Yeah, recuperating with her," Guppy added.

Razor gave them his infamous stare, and they went back to playing pool. "Beer," he said to Avery, the female bartender.

"I heard you got a new girl, Razor," Avery said. "Patterson's daughter?" She opened the bottle and gave it to him.

He sat at the bar and drank his beer. Guppy couldn't leave it alone and came over to slap him on the back. "What happened, buddy? Did she realize she was slumming and went back to her Porsche-driving doctors?"

Razor was used to the guys teasing him. It was part of the culture. They all joked with one another. But this time it bothered him. He downed the beer in two large gulps and gave Guppy a look and a growl that sent him back to the pool table, this time for good. Razor turned his gaze to Avery, and she brought him another beer. "Shot," he said.

Avery complied and watched him down it. "You walked out on her, didn't you?" she said softly. "Having second thoughts?" He pointed to the shot glass, indicating that he wanted another. She refilled it, and he downed that one too. "Call her and apologize."

"No," he said.

Avery shook her head. "You're making a mistake." She knew the regulars who came into the bar. She had been working there for five years and was a comanager. But Avery had a rule and never dated the guys who frequented the place. That was why they respected her and talked to her.

"My mistake to make," he said.

*****

Razor sat there for hours drinking his beers. Teflon walked into the bar and immediately knew something was wrong. He took pride in knowing his men, and he believed that being a good leader also meant being a father, brother, or friend.

"Hi, Avery. How long has he been sitting there?" Teflon knew that Razor stood at the bar when he was talking to someone. The only times he saw him sit at the bar was when he was with Eve that first time or when something was bothering him. Otherwise, he'd be at the team table or playing pool.

"Since about two thirty or so. Did two shots right away." She handed Teflon a beer.

"I'm guessing he hasn't eaten, so get some food in him. On me." Teflon knew Razor would approach him if he wanted to talk. He wasn't ready, so Teflon went to the pool table where Guppy was still messing around.

Razor ordered another shot. He kept going over it in his mind. She went out with him three times. After golf, the dinner date, and she invited him over after the deployment. She approached him at the clubhouse. *Why?* Quietly, he said, "Doesn't make sense. I'm a door-kicker."

Avery placed a hamburger and fries in front of him. "This is from Teflon. Eat something."

He growled but picked up the burger and took a bite. He cleaned his plate and nodded at Teflon, who was now sitting at the team table with another team member.

Half an hour later, a woman bumped his arm. "Hi there, big guy. Care to buy a girl a drink?"

"No," Razor told her.

"He wants to be alone. Move along, please," Avery told her. She looked out for the guys when they got like this.

"Oh, come on. Get some of your buddies and join my friends." She pointed to a table of three giggling women who were in their mid-twenties. They were holding mixed drinks and had on beach apparel beneath cropped T-shirts and short shorts that made them look like tourists. "We'll have fun."

"Hey—" Avery started but was interrupted by a short-tempered and drunk Razor.

He stood to his full six-foot-five-inch height and said, "I'd rather hump a camel." Then he slowly walked out to his truck.

"Bastard!" the woman yelled at him.

"Razor! Hey, Razor!" Teflon caught up to him. "You were supposed to be taking it easy today. I hope you aren't taking your pain meds while drinking."

"No."

"Are you OK to drive?" Teflon asked. "Look at me." Razor reached into his pocket and gave Teflon his keys. "Let's go, big guy." Teflon had to remind Razor to put his seat belt on. He hoped that Razor would talk to him as they drove, but he didn't. He just stared out the window. Then he closed his eyes. Teflon saw him jerk awake a few times. When it happened again, he asked about it. "Nightmare?"

"Uh, yeah."

"Mission related or personal?"

Razor looked out the passenger window. "Mission."

"That's normal. We all get them sometimes. It got hairy on that last one. More than usual. But you did well. You always do. You've been a great leader to the pups. Guppy looks up to you. That kid has potential."

"You said that about me. Remember?"

"Yeah. I was right." Teflon wasn't going to ask for details about the nightmare. Razor would tell him if he wanted to. "If you need to vent, I'm here. Mission related or even personal."

"Thanks, Boss," Razor said.

Teflon pulled into the parking lot, and they walked to Razor's apartment. Razor swayed a bit on the way.

"Thanks again, Boss."

Teflon smacked him on the back. "No problem. Battle buddies on and off the field, right?" Razor grunted. "Drink some water or Gatorade and rest. See you later."

"Boss?" Razor flopped down on his couch.

"Yeah?"

"You ever date a girl you thought was better than you?"

Teflon smiled, then sat down. "Yeah. They were all better than me. Even the ex-wife."

Razor leaned his head back and sighed. "I screwed up. Got caught sneaking out like a fox leaving the henhouse."

"Why did you leave?"

"I don't know. I've never stayed."

Teflon sighed. "She's different, Razor. I don't know her, but she seems down to earth. I mean, hell, she was willing to go out with you."

"I don't get that. Why me?"

"Why not you? You're a good guy. You've taught these youngsters a thing or two about manners. You're serving your country with an honorable job. Why not you?"

"I'm just a frogman. She's a respectable woman."

"Sounds like you have a personal problem. I may not know her, but I'll tell you this. If you want a relationship with her, you need to stop thinking she's a socialite. She's not. She comes from people like us. Her dad was a diver. Her mom was a substitute teacher. Stop berating yourself."

Razor was tired and kept falling asleep. Teflon hit him on the leg. "What!"

"Get some rest." Teflon called for a ride and left.

Razor went to the fridge and pulled out a large bottle of Gatorade. He drank it and then went to bed.

CHAPTER 4

When Razor woke the next morning, he went to the fridge and downed another large bottle of Gatorade. After a workout and a shower, he did some laundry and puttered around the apartment. He checked his wound, then cleaned it and put on a fresh bandage. Putting the load of clothes away, he decided to go to the beach to blow off some steam. Razor changed into his swim shorts, threw his surfboard into the back of his truck, and drove to his favorite spot on Virginia Beach.

It was a little overcast and had drizzled some, but it was warm, and the waves were good enough for him to surf. Razor had placed a piece of plastic wrap over the gauze bandage to keep it from getting too wet. Regular water was OK, but he didn't want an infection from the ocean water. He also needed to be careful and not tear his stitches. He paddled out and waited for a wave. Catching a decent-size one, he rode it in. Falling off, he paddled out again. He repeated this process a few more times.

*****

The next time he paddled out, he just sat on the board, his legs dangling in the water. The sun was coming out, and he looked up and closed his eyes. The heat felt good on his face. He rode one more wave in and then carried the board and set it on the sand. He stretched gently, checking his side. No blood on the gauze, and the plastic wrap was still in place. Razor sat down on his beach towel and then leaned back, closing his eyes.

As he soaked up the sun, he recalled the look on Eve's face when she caught him trying to leave her condo. She didn't deserve that. He could have stayed. Why didn't he? *She liked you and you liked her. You treated her like just another . . .* He realized what an ass he'd been and how he'd let his own insecurities get in the way of his relationship with her. "Live and learn, jackass. You'll probably never see her again," he mumbled as he sat up and collected his things.

He decided to go to the bar and hang out. Stepping out of his truck, he put on his T-shirt. He thought about changing into his sneakers but decided to leave his flip-flops on. He really didn't care if the guys teased him. He wasn't in the mood to care about what they thought.

"Been surfing, Razor?" Avery asked when he walked in.

"Yeah."

"Nice day. How were the waves?" She handed him a beer.

"Small," he said as he looked around. He sat at the bar, and Avery shook her head. "What?"

"Nothing," she said. She knew he was still thinking about Eve Patterson.

He drank his beers. No shots, just beers and a water he sipped every once in a while. His phone buzzed, and he looked at it. He was hoping for a mission to distract him, but it was her. He set it down on the bar, letting it go to voicemail. But she didn't leave a message. He peeled the label from his bottle and didn't notice when she walked in. She ordered a beer and sat at the opposite end of the bar.

"You're Patterson, right?" Avery asked.

"Yes. Eve Patterson."

"I'm glad you didn't give up on him." She motioned toward Razor.

"What makes you think I'm here about him?" Eve asked.

Avery smiled. "No offense, but I don't think you'd be here without a reason." She wiped the bar with her towel as she spoke. "I've worked here for five years, and I know our clientele. I also know you're Chief Patterson's daughter, but you've never been here until you came in with him, right?"

"I'll admit that the last time I was here was with my father. After his retirement ceremony," Eve told her.

"Razor is a good guy, and he knows he screwed up."

"I need to talk to him." Eve had to know why he left. If anything, she wanted to tell him how he made her feel. She wasn't going to let any man walk out on her without an explanation.

"Good luck," Avery said before moving down the bar to help a customer.

Eve sat on her stool, avoiding Razor's eyes. She nursed her beer as he peeled the label off his third. He still hadn't noticed her. Fifteen minutes later, a server brought out two plates of burgers and fries. Avery took one and placed it in front of Razor. "What the hell, Avery? I didn't order—"

"Stand down, sasquatch. It's from her." She pointed to Eve, who took a bite of her burger.

Razor looked at her stoically.

"Don't be an idiot, Razor. She's making an effort," Avery said. "You owe her an explanation."

He made a noise, then looked at the burger and picked it up. Every once in a while, he glanced at her. She looked so out of place. She was dressed in a suit with a starched shirt and had her hair pulled back in a ponytail. *God, she's hot.* Even in a suit, he wanted her. His stomach did a flip as he thought about making love to her. Putting his hands on her body and touching her smooth skin. Those lips were so soft. The first two buttons on her dress shirt were undone, revealing just enough to skirt the line between professional and sexy. His eyes lingered there while he imagined opening that next button. Moving his finger down her cleavage and then cupping her breast. *Oh my God!* She was driving him crazy.

"What do you say, Razor, another beer?" Avery asked, bringing him back to the present.

Avery had startled him, and a fry went down the wrong pipe. He coughed a few times. He finished his beer, and when he stopped coughing, he said, "Yeah, send her one too."

"Attaboy." Avery smiled. She took his plate away and grabbed two more beers. "He's softening," Avery told Eve as she placed another beer on the bar. "By the way, I'm Avery."

"Eve. Thank you."

"You aren't a government agent, are you?" Avery asked.

Eve laughed. "No. I'm a Realtor. Is that what I look like?"

"A little. But I really didn't think you were a G-woman."

"I'm in the office today. I don't always wear suits. It just depends."

Razor watched as Avery spoke to her. Then Avery went to wait on another customer, and he saw a guy approach Eve. He was on another team, and they had just returned from a mission.

"Hi, haven't seen you before. But I was out of town. I'm Chad," he said.

"Hi," Eve said, being polite.

Razor watched as they engaged in small talk. He didn't like it, but he continued to watch them.

Avery sighed and shook her head. "Why do I help these guys?" she mumbled to herself. Walking over to Razor, she reached over the bar and punched him in the arm. "Get over there, sasquatch. She came here for you."

Razor narrowed his eyes at her for the punch. Adjusting his ball cap, he stood up, grabbed his beer, and walked to Eve.

Chad stopped talking when Razor approached. Razor didn't have to say anything. He just stared at Chad.

"Uh, hey, Razor. What's up?" Chad asked.

"Pound sand," Razor told him.

Chad sighed. Razor was on a different team, but they knew each other. One thing everyone knew was that you didn't mess with Razor. Chad respected Razor and backed off. "Sorry, I didn't know. Nice talking to you, Eve," he said and walked back to his buddies.

"That wasn't very nice," Eve said, sipping her beer.

Razor stood next to her. "Yeah, I'm a jerk. And I was a jerk two days ago."

"Is that an apology?" Eve asked him.

"Yeah." He felt bad and didn't really know what else to say to her. Razor didn't feel like getting into a deep conversation there at the bar.

"Why did you leave?" she asked.

"I always leave."

Eve sighed. She expected a better answer than that. "I see. So I was just another—" She started to rise from her barstool.

He placed his hand on her arm to stop her. "No, you aren't. I'm sorry, and I regret leaving without telling you."

"So you would have woken me and left?"

"I . . . uh . . ." Is that what he meant? That sounded just as bad. Waking her to say he was leaving. "No, I—"

"Just tell me, please. I really thought we were getting along. I like you and want to get to know you."

"We're just . . . different." He sat down.

"No, we're not. My dad was an enlisted diver. My mom stayed home with us until my brother and I got older. She was a substitute teacher sometimes. I got a scholarship to college and have worked hard to get where I am today. You've worked hard in your job. We're not that different."

This isn't what he wanted, but it couldn't be avoided. "You drive a BMW, and I drive a truck."

"It impresses my clients. But I won't lie, I like it."

His eyes darted to her wrist. He could barely see her watch under the cuff of her shirt. He sighed.

"What? Tell me."

He moved his hand to her wrist and pulled up the cuff. "Just as I thought. A Rolex."

"So?"

"You make more money than me," he finally said.

She shook her head. "Wow." Standing up, she said, "You backward-thinking, chauvinistic Neanderthal!" Some of the others in the bar looked over at them, but Eve didn't care about making a scene. That's what it came down to. Money. He couldn't handle the fact that she made more than him.

She pulled her wallet from her purse, but Avery yelled at her. "Your money's no good here, Patterson."

Eve threw down a ten-dollar tip, which was more than enough, and walked out the door. But just outside she paused. As angry as he'd just made her, she still wanted him. Ever since he'd left the other night, she couldn't get him out of her thoughts. It was his problem, his hang-up. Money.

As Eve stood outside the bar, in that moment she felt his touch on her arm and the way he kissed her. Her eyes closed, and she thought about that night. His lips on hers. The way he wrapped his arms around her and made her feel safe. His hand gently and slowly running up her leg while he kissed her neck. Touching her waist, her hip, moving down to . . .

"You're not getting off that easy, Zack Reston." With fire in her eyes and a new sense of determination, she strode back into the bar. Still sitting in the same spot, she looked at Razor, placed her hands on his cheeks, and kissed him with all the passion she had from that night. She gently bit his lip as she pulled away. "I bite too," she said fiercely, referring to the patch on his hat. Then she turned and strode out.

He stared at her and kept staring even after she was gone. Everyone in the bar was looking at Razor, waiting to see what would happen next.

"Razor! Get off your ass and go after her," Avery said.

Razor growled at Avery. "I'm getting tired of your orders." Then he stood and walked out.

Eve was leaning against her SUV and looked at her watch. "Took you long enough," she said.

He wrapped his arms around her and lifted her up as he kissed her.

CHAPTER 5

Razor and Eve were eating at a restaurant when a man approached their table. "Eve? Yeah, I thought that was you." He was well dressed in an expensive suit.

"Hello, Rich. How are you?"

"Great. You know, you never did take me up on that offer of seeing my sailboat."

Eve thought it was rude of him to say that in front of Razor. "Rich, this is—"

"Razor," he said, interrupting Eve. Razor stood and extended his hand. "Nice to meet you."

"This is Rich Williams," Eve said, finishing the introduction.

Rich had kept his focus on Eve, but when he turned to Razor, his eyes met him at his chin. Moving his gaze up to meet Razor's, he narrowed his eyes slightly in disapproval. "Yeah, hi," Rich said, dismissing him. "Razor?" He scowled. "What the hell kind of name is that?"

The look and his attitude were not lost on Razor, who was not very pleased with the situation. Razor began to speak, but Rich turned back to Eve. "So about my boat. Would you be up to coming out for a sail?"

Razor couldn't believe it. *Did he just ask Eve out in front of me?*

"No, thank you. I'm involved with someone," Eve told him.

Razor was so engrossed in Rich while trying not to lose his temper that didn't notice that Eve was looking at him and smiling.

But Rich did. "Really?" he asked. It was if he couldn't believe that someone like Eve would date this large gorilla of a man. "Well, maybe another time." He walked away without another word.

Razor wasn't happy, and his anger was growing. He sat back down and tried to stay calm.

"Zack? I'm sorry about that."

"Forget it," he said. But he couldn't let it go. He was even quieter than usual through the rest of dinner.

Razor paid the bill, and they left the restaurant. Walking beside him, Eve tried to hold his hand, but he moved it up to scratch his beard. He also walked slightly to the right, increasing the gap between them. Reaching in his pocket, he took out his key fob and unlocked the truck. His upbringing and manners wouldn't allow her to open the vehicle's door herself, so he quickly did it for her.

"Is something wrong?" Eve asked.

"No," he said as he closed her door. Starting the truck, he drove back to her condo.

"Zack, he was rude, and I'm sorry about that. I told him we were seeing each other."

Razor took a deep breath and replied, "No, you said you were involved with someone."

"Yes, and I was looking at you when I said it." Eve's voice was slightly raised. "He took the hint and left."

Razor felt she should have been more specific. After a minute of silence, he said, "We never said we were exclusive. Doesn't matter. I'll be gone soon."

Eve looked at him in disbelief. "What do you mean, you'll be gone?"

"I'm retiring and going home. To Texas."

Now it was Eve's turn to be angry. "You're just now telling me?"

"Going home wasn't my original plan. I have to go back because my dad isn't doing well." He spoke loudly.

Feeling badly, she said calmly, "I'm sorry about your father." She looked out the passenger window. She had questions but couldn't speak as she felt the pit in her stomach expand. Not wanting him to see the tears forming in her eyes, Eve kept her head turned toward the window. *Leaving. He's leaving me.* She had feelings for him and wanted a relationship.

Now he tells her he's leaving. Eve was hurt, angry, and sad all at the same time.

Razor parked and began to get out, but Eve opened the door and said quickly, "Just stay here. Goodbye . . . Razor."

"Eve, I—" Razor wanted to explain about his dad. He also was willing to talk to her about how he felt about what happened at the restaurant concerning Rich. But it was too late. He should have spoken to her in the truck. Instead, he kept his mouth shut, and now she was gone. Half in and half out of his truck, he said, "Idiot, you did it again." Then he realized she'd called him Razor. *I guess it's really over.* He hadn't meant to tell her he was leaving like that. His plan was to break it to her gently. He leaned his head against the steering wheel.

*****

Eve ran up the stairs to her condo. By the time she was in front of her door, she couldn't see through her tears. She fumbled in her purse for her keys and dropped them. Picking them up, Eve wiped her eyes and managed to open the door. As soon as she was inside, she closed the door and locked it. The alarm system was beeping, but she barely heard it. Seconds later her phone buzzed; it was the alarm company. She reset the alarm and answered the phone, giving the caller her security password so that they knew she was all right and that there wasn't a problem.

Kimberly A. Biggerstaff © 2025

But there was a problem. Zack Reston. She had fallen in love, and he had just broken her heart.

*****

The next two weeks were miserable for Razor, but he was so busy that he didn't have time to think about it. Things moved quickly, and before he knew it, he was leaving the next day. It was his last day at the Rally Point. He was going to miss this place.

Razor walked into the bar as he had so many times before. But this time was different. He heard the bell ring and stopped in his tracks.

"Look who finally decided to grace us with his presence," Wayne said from behind the bar. "Zachary Wyatt Reston, senior chief petty officer, *retired*!"

Everyone in the bar had stopped what they were doing and stared at him. The newly retired man glanced around the room at his buddies, all of whom were looking at him. He slowly raised his hand, pointing a finger in the air. They all watched with anticipation. He gave a quiet growl and moved his arm in a circular motion. It was the hand signal for rally point. But in this bar, it meant a round for the house on him. Wayne rang the bell, and everyone cheered. Razor growled again and walked over to his now former team members, Nugget, Guppy, and Tigger, sitting at their table.

Before he sat down, one of the servers, Misty, walked over and said, "Congratulations, Razor." She smiled and gave him a big kiss on the cheek. Misty had been working at the Rally Point for a year while taking college classes. She was friendly, outgoing, and knew all the regulars, including Razor. She had a boyfriend stationed at the base, so the men looked after her if someone new came in and got too handsy.

"Do I have to retire to get that, Misty?" asked Nugget.

"You'll never get that, Nugget," Misty said, winking at him.

The men laughed, and Misty released Razor to get the beers he had just bought. Razor sat at the wooden table. Misty returned with a tray of beers and a round of whiskey shots for the four men. Razor looked at her.

"The whiskeys are on me, Razor," Guppy said. He held up his shot in a toast. "To a great friend, mentor, and teammate. Thank you, Razor. *Hoorah!*"

"Hoorah!" everyone called in response and drank the shot.

"So, Razor, are you finally going to tell us what you're going to do now that you're retired?" Tigger asked. They all waited. But before Razor said anything, another man walked over and set his hand on Razor's shoulder. Everyone stood up.

"Sit down, fellas." It was Teflon, who'd been temporarily moved to help out another team.

"Thanks for coming," Razor said, shaking his hand. They were the first words he'd spoken since he'd entered the establishment.

"I wouldn't miss it, Razor. Congratulations," Teflon said.

"They keeping you busy, Command Master Chief Tefflack?" Nugget asked.

"Always. Good to see everyone." Misty brought him his beer, and he took a sip immediately. "Razor, did you even shave for your ceremony?"

The guys laughed. As a young man, Razor was always getting in trouble because it looked like he never shaved. He had a five o'clock shadow at noon. When he joined his first SEAL team, he was given the nickname Razor, along with a seabag full of disposable razors. Two days after his retirement ceremony, his beard was full again. Razor was dressed in tactical pants and a T-shirt with US NAVY RETIRED written on it. It had been a gift from one of the guys. He wore his favorite ball cap with the patch that read YES, I DO BITE.

"So what's next, Razor?" one of the guys asked.

"Home," Razor said in his deep, gruff voice.

"Now that you're retired, you think we could get more than a grunt and one- or two-word sentences?" said another.

"Hey, who was that woman that almost shot your old teammate, Dicky? We should have invited her. What was her name?" Nugget asked. Razor had told the story more than once of the time Sam Barrett had quickly taken a handgun from him and shot a lightbulb out that was hanging over Dicky from about twenty feet away. He had mistakenly commented that she probably barely qualified with her weapon. Then she threw a knife dead-center in a playing card, also near Dicky.

"Barrett," Razor said. Samantha Barrett was a retired air force officer whom Razor and his team helped on an agency mission years before. She had already gained his respect before that, having seen her strength and courage on the battlefield in Afghanistan, which earned her a Silver Star. Her daughter had written a book about her life, and Razor had read it.

"Yeah, Barrett. You ever talk to her?"

Razor grunted and half smiled. That was all he did. The others waited for something more, but Razor was just being himself.

"Barrett even made him laugh," Teflon said.

Razor reminisced about that operation and others. The younger SEALs also spoke of their missions with Razor. At times they threw out the word *redacted* because all their missions were classified and they needed to be careful when they spoke about them in public. No one brought up Eve. They knew something had happened between them, so no one asked. An hour later, when there was a lull in the conversation, Razor said, "Willis, Texas."

"What?" Nugget asked.

"Home. Willis, Texas."

"Where is that, and why?" Guppy asked.

"North of Houston. Parents are old," Razor said.

"Well, good luck, buddy. Keep in touch," Guppy told him.

Each of his team members slapped him on the back and shook his hand at some point throughout the evening. A few more women came over and kissed him. Some he didn't know and were drunk. The younger single guys were jealous of the attention and teased him about it. Razor couldn't help but think about Eve. He missed her and wished he'd invited her. As if on cue, he heard a familiar voice.

"Hello, Zack," a woman said, appearing behind him as he leaned on the bar. He turned and straightened up as he looked at her and smiled.

"Eve."

"I hope you weren't going to leave without saying goodbye," she said.

"No." Actually, he wasn't sure if he would have stopped to see her. He wanted to. He didn't like the way things went when they last saw each other.

"I'm sorry," they said in unison and then laughed.

"How did you know to come here?" Razor asked.

"I received a call from Guppy."

Razor looked over at Guppy sitting at the team table, and their eyes met. Razor nodded a silent thank-you, and Guppy raised his beer. "How did he get your number?"

"He called my office. Said he was tired of seeing you mope around like a sad puppy dog," she teased.

"Did not."

"No, he didn't."

"Eve, may I get you a drink?" Avery asked.

"Yes, on me," Razor said quickly.

"Thank you. I'll have a beer," Eve said.

Razor had so much he wanted to tell her, but he remained quiet. It wasn't until Avery brought her beer and she took a sip that Razor spoke up. He leaned down and whispered, "Can I have a moment?"

They walked to a corner away from the crowd. Shoving his hands in his front pockets, he began. "Eve, I'm sorry for telling you like that. I was angry with the way that guy was acting. I had other plans. A different way of telling you I was leaving."

"I'm sorry for the way I acted. You just caught me off guard. You never said you were retiring."

"I know. Maybe I should have brought it up sooner. I'm just . . . I never had anyone I wanted to share things with. I should have told you what was going on. I'm sorry."

Razor was about to kiss her when Nugget slapped him on the back and said, "Time to pay up, Razor. Grog bowl!"

"Hoorah!" everyone yelled. Nugget pushed Razor toward a wall that had camouflage netting on it and a brand-new toilet bowl sitting on some pallets. It was lined with a garbage bag and filled with an unknown liquid. The grog bowl is a tradition at a military dining-in. There are certain things that are said during the ceremony, but they kept things casual tonight.

"We'll forgo the formalities. Dish it out, you retired BTF—big tough frogman!" Nugget told him as Guppy handed Razor a red Solo cup and a metal ladle.

Razor took the ladle and reached into the toilet bowl, pulling up the dark-brown liquid and pouring it into the cup. He poured more for Guppy, Nugget, Tigger, and Teflon and anyone else who wanted to partake. He began to raise his glass when Eve caught his eye. He poured one more and handed it to her.

"She's a civilian," Tigger said.

Razor growled at him. "Her dad is on the wall."

"OK," he said, as if his opinion mattered.

They all raised their cups, and it became quiet. "To the president of the United States!" Razor shouted.

"To the president!" the others responded.

They drank, and everyone made a face at the concoction. Eve remembered when her father retired and those in attendance did the same thing. But she didn't participate that time. She pursed her lips after forcing the liquid down her throat.

"To the United States Navy!" Razor yelled.

"To the navy!" everyone repeated.

They drank.

"To the admiral of the navy!"

"To the admiral!"

They drank.

"To our fallen comrades!"

"To our fallen comrades!"

They drank.

"To the frogmen!"

"To the frogmen!"

They drank.

"To Retired Senior Chief Petty Officer Reston!"

"Screw him!" the guys yelled and drank. The others in the bar who didn't participate watched the ceremony and hollered and cheered.

"Gauntlet!" someone yelled.

Guppy, Nugget, Tigger, Teflon, and others made two lines facing each other. Normally this was done when an enlisted person received a promotion and was wearing their new stripes. Razor stood at one end and took a step. Each person on either side punched Razor in the arm and congratulated him. He took a step and again received his punches. This continued until he reached the end of the line. Eve had a smirk on her face as she stood in front of him.

"They said I had to do this," she said as she pushed a tin pie plate of whipped cream in his face. More cheers and hollering. Razor took it all in stride. He wiped the whipped cream out of his eyes and smiled at her. She reached up and ran her finger in the cream along his face. Then she seductively put it in her mouth. Razor's face went from smiling to serious.

Damn, that was hot. "Don't do that," he told her, looking around.

"Do what?"

"That. That thing with your finger."

She reached up and wiped more whipped cream, but this time she held in front of his mouth, teasing him. Tempting him. He reached up, gently took her hand, and put it down. "That's not funny." She was getting him all hot and bothered.

Avery handed Razor a towel. "Patterson, I didn't think you had it in you. Good job." She laughed.

"You were messing with me," Razor said, wiping his face.

"Yes and no." The corner of her mouth raised. Changing the subject she said, "What was in that grog thing?"

He was still thinking about sucking the whipped cream off her finger. That was something he'd love to do in private. He was still staring at her blankly.

"Zack?"

"What? Oh, uh, only the bartenders know. They make it up for us. Nasty, huh?" Razor said.

"Not my favorite cocktail," Eve answered. "Thank you for including me." Then she punched him in the arm.

"Ow. I'd prefer something else from you." He grinned.

"Oh yeah? Like what?"

"A kiss."

"Here? In front of your friends?" Eve was playing coy.

"Maybe."

Eve lifted her hand and, with her finger, motioned for him to come nearer.

Razor stepped close and leaned down as Eve gave him the most romantic and passionate kiss anyone had ever seen—a Hollywood end-of-the-movie kiss. Razor's stomach somersaulted and swarmed with butterflies, and his heart stopped beating. After what seemed like forever, they parted.

Razor took a deep breath as he gazed into Eve's eyes. He didn't see anyone else or hear anything. "Eve, w—" He was interrupted by Tigger, who accidentally bumped into him.

"Sorry, dude. Got to go home. Take care of yourself," Tigger said, giving him a hug.

"Keep your head on a swivel and best of luck with the baby. Email me a photo," Razor told him.

"You bet. I hope we'll still see you around, Eve."

"Take care, Tigger."

Nugget appeared and handed Razor and Eve each a beer. Guppy pulled Eve toward the pool table. "Come on, I want a game."

The moment was gone, and Razor watched as Eve glanced back and smiled at him. He looked around at his friends, all laughing and having a good time. He was going to miss them.

CHAPTER 6

Three hours after Razor arrived, he said goodbye to his buddies, friends, and teammates. Taking Eve's hand, they walked out of the bar and to her SUV.

There was a gentle breeze, and he moved some strands of hair out of her face. He was nervous and didn't want to assume anything.

"Your place?" Razor asked. He was prepared if she said no. But all those feelings he had for her were back, and he really wanted to spend the night with her. The entire night. Wake up with her in his arms.

"Why not yours? I've never seen it."

"Packed. No bed."

She laughed. "And you're probably not in a hotel. Sleeping on the floor with a sleeping bag, right?" He shrugged. Eve had learned so much about him during their short time together. She knew him better than some of his teammates. He'd opened up to her more than anyone else. "Zack, what are we going to do with you? Follow me home unless you can't drive."

"I can drive." He placed a hand around her waist and pulled her in for a kiss. Starting off gentle, he deepened the kiss. Her lips were so soft and he wanted the moment to last as long as possible. He ran his hand down the small of her back, over the belt on her jeans, and let it rest on her ass. His other hand was holding hers. Their fingers intertwined. "Do you have whipped cream?" he asked when they parted.

The feelings came back for her as well. She was speechless. It was amazing what a kiss could do. Her legs felt weak, and her heart was pounding. Eve's chest was heaving and she was breathless. "I . . . uh . . . think . . . so." She managed to smile and got into her vehicle.

Razor followed Eve to her condo, knowing the way like the back of his hand. He trailed her up the stairs, waiting as she unlocked the door. Once inside, she handed him a beer. He took it and walked to her balcony, which overlooked the ocean. He loved this view and would miss it. He'd spent most of his career in the Virginia Beach area, more than other deployments and time on ships. Closing his eyes, he smelled the ocean and heard the waves below. There was a light wind, and it felt good.

"Zack? Penny for your thoughts," Eve said, standing next to him with a glass of wine.

"Just taking it in. One last time." The others would have laughed at him for being sentimental. Not Eve. He could drop his guard with her and show a side of himself that others rarely saw. Razor shared things with her that he normally wouldn't. Like the tattoo on his arm. When someone asked about it, he just said it was Neptune and he liked the trident. That's all. Eve asked questions and prodded him to get more information. She did it in a way that Zack didn't mind. Eve just had a way of making him talk to her. Good thing she wasn't an interrogator. He'd give her the nuclear codes, if he knew them.

What did Eve see in him? She had a master's degree and a six-figure salary. He'd earned his bachelor's degree while serving, but he was still just a man who killed the bad guys. She drove a BMW and wore a Rolex and Ralph Lauren. He kept telling himself they were different. She never liked it when he said that. She told him he was more than just a door-kicker.

Razor had also wondered why she wasn't married by now. He knew there were plenty of men out there waiting for a woman like Eve—smart, successful, and beautiful. She was five foot nine and had long light-brown hair with red highlights. When the light hit her hair just right, you could see the red strands. She'd told him her grandmother had red hair and that's where she'd inherited it from. Not to mention those green eyes that reminded him of his woobie. He smiled thinking about when he'd told her that. It was funny now.

He looked at her. "Emeralds," he said.

She turned toward him. "What?"

"Your eyes are like emeralds. It's what I should have said."

"No. That's nice but predictable. Cliché. I will always remember that you compared them to a color in your woobie." Her smile faded. "Going back to Texas?" she asked, knowing he was.

"Yeah. It's the right thing to do," he told her.

"How's your father?"

"I had to call my sister to get the truth. She saw him a couple of months ago and said he's weak and gets tired a lot. He's worked hard his whole life."

"I'm sorry." Eve placed an arm around his waist and changed the subject. "You'll be missed, Zack."

"The guys will forget about me in a couple of weeks."

"Maybe they will. But I'm not talking about them." She looked up at the big man. He wrapped his arms around her and leaned down, brushing his lips with hers. Her lips were still soft, and he smiled when he pulled away from her. "What are you smiling at?" she asked.

"Nothing. I always enjoy kissing you." He gazed into her eyes and kissed her again. Then he surprised himself and said, "Come with me to Texas. You can sell condos and houses anywhere."

"What? Zack, I—"

The look on her face told him what he needed to know. "Forget it. I was just messing with you. You wouldn't like Texas anyway. Too many backward-thinking Neanderthal cows out there." He laughed.

She laughed too. But she thought about what he'd asked. He'd caught her off guard. She didn't know what to say. In the back of her mind, she would love to go with him. But the reality was that her business was thriving. If she left, it would mean starting over. She'd spent years networking, building a base clientele, and learning the market in the Norfolk and Virginia Beach area. She just wasn't ready to pick up and leave.

*****

They stared out at the ocean. It was a perfect night. There was a slight breeze, and a full moon illuminated the sky. Suddenly, Razor had a thought. He pulled his phone out and looked at Eve. "Turn around," he said. "I want a picture of us."

He flipped the screen so that he could take a selfie. "Smile." He held out his arm, and when he was satisfied, he pressed the circle three times.

"Take another," Eve said. When he was ready, she kissed him on the cheek at just the right time.

Razor smiled and looked at the pictures with her. "Stand there," he said as he backed away.

"What are you doing?"

"I want one of you. Just you."

"That's not a good background. It's too dark," Eve told him.

"Just let me take it. Smile."

Eve relented. "Finished?"

"Yeah. Thanks."

"Text me those, will you?"

"Already did."

They reached for their drinks on the small table, and their hands touched. Goose bumps appeared on Eve's skin and she felt a tingling sensation. Smiling at each other, they sipped their respective beverages. Eve sat on one of the lounge chairs and looked at Razor.

"You're watching me," Razor said, still staring at the ocean.

"Yes, I am."

Razor turned to her. "Would you like more wine?"

"Yes."

"I'll get it," he said. He took her glass and went to the kitchen. After pouring her wine, he opened the fridge and retrieved a beer for himself. Grinning, he grabbed the can of whipped cream.

"Are you OK, Zack?" Eve called when it seemed like it was taking him too long. What was he doing?

"Yeah. Be right there."

Eve waited and then took the glass when it appeared from behind her. Then Razor stepped beside her. Eve almost dropped her glass. He wore nothing but his boxer shorts. His beard was covered in whipped cream, and there was a whipped cream arrow on his chest pointing toward the boxer shorts.

"I saw this on a TV show."

"That's . . . uh . . ." Eve was speechless but wore a big smile.

"Would you do that thing again?"

Eve smiled and took a sip of her wine. "What thing?" She knew what he was talking about but wanted him to say it.

"With your finger."

Eve stood up and stepped very close to him. Slowly, she ran her finger halfway down the arrow. Feeling her stroke his chest felt so good. He smiled at her as his body warmed to her touch. Then she took her finger and held it front of him. She pressed it to his lips and gave him an inviting look. Raising an eyebrow, he licked the whipped cream from her finger. She watched as his tongue slowly traced one side and then the other. He took it into his mouth, then grinned as he released her finger, now cleaned of whipped cream.

Eve swallowed as her chest heaved. She placed her finger back on his torso and slowly made her way to the end of the arrow, just above his boxer shorts. She brought her finger close to her mouth, teasing Razor. Then she licked it seductively, running her tongue up one side and down the other before placing it in her mouth.

Unable to wait, Razor went to grab her, but she stepped back and removed her finger, shaking it. "Not yet," she whispered. "Stay here." She found the whipped cream. Returning to him, she shook the can and walked behind him. He shivered when she sprayed a small amount on his shoulder. He felt her lips kiss him and then her tongue as she licked the whipped cream. Then she sprayed his other shoulder. Again, Eve kissed him and licked the whipped cream. The next spray was at the small of his back. Razor wasn't sure how much more he could take. He felt her hands run along his back. Then her fingers trailed down lightly to the whipped cream. Her tongue licked and teased him.

"You've been a naughty boy, Zachary. Let's get you cleaned up," she said as she faced him, running a hand along his bare back and shoulders to his chest. Thinking she was in control, Razor surprised her by sweeping her up in his arms and carrying her to the bedroom.

*****

After making love and falling asleep in his arms, Eve woke. Her thoughts immediately turned to what Razor had asked the night before. "Zack? Are you awake?"

"Yeah." He squeezed her as they lay in bed.

"What time do you have to leave?"

"I'm not really on a schedule. I was going to leave sometime today."

"Why are you going to Texas?" She turned and looked up at him.

"I told you, to help my parents. My brother and sister live in other cities. Dad's having a tough time keeping up with the stupid cows he has."

She smiled at him. "You're a good son, Zachary." Eve ran a hand over the arm that held her. She felt safe and comfortable. "About what you said last night."

"Forget it. I understand. You have a life and a business here. I was just caught up in the moment. Let's just enjoy this."

Without knowing it, he messed up again. He'd already dismissed a conversation Eve was willing to have. He wanted to move on. She closed her eyes and decided to move on as well. "Spend the day with me. At least a few hours, please."

Razor smiled. "Let's go to the beach, and I'll take you to lunch."

"I'd like that."

*****

Razor knew the longer he stayed with her, the harder it would be to leave. They showered and dressed after eating a light breakfast. Razor found his swim trunks packed in a duffel bag, and after changing, Eve told him he could drive her SUV. His truck was packed full. All he had to do was go back to his apartment and place the few remaining items in the small U-Haul trailer, then he could leave for Texas.

*****

They walked to the beach and found a place to put their towels. Eve had packed a few bottles of water and set the small cooler down next to her towel. Razor pulled his shirt off and dropped it on his towel. He watched as Eve slipped off her shorts and shirt to reveal her bikini, and he whistled.

Eve smiled. "Thank you." She put some sunblock on and handed him the bottle. He sprayed it on her back first, then rubbed it over her. His hand moved slowly over her back, as he enjoyed touching her smooth skin. She was only a couple of years younger than him at thirty-seven, but she could pass for thirty. He could tell she took care of herself. His thoughts wandered back to last night and making love to her.

"Zack? Zack!"

"What?"

"I think you got it, thanks. Your turn."

"Sorry, yeah." He gave her the bottle, and she sprayed the lotion onto his muscular back and rubbed it in.

She was curious about the two other small tattoos he had. "The razor blade on your arm I understand. What's this thumbs-up on your shoulder?"

Kimberly A. Biggerstaff © 2025

"Gig 'em, Aggies. For Texas A&M University." Remembering she told him she graduated from Brown University, he asked, "What's the mascot for Brown?"

"A brown bear, of course. Named Bruno."

"Our official mascot is a collie named Reveille." Razor turned and kissed her. He took her hand, and they walked to the water.

After playfully frolicking like kids, Razor grabbed Eve and kissed her again. A beach ball landed near Eve, and a little boy wearing a life vest ran through the water to retrieve it. He couldn't have been more than three years old. Eve picked up the ball and carried it toward him so that he wouldn't get too far from his father, who was chasing after him.

Razor watched as Eve smiled and handed him the inflatable ball. "Here you go. Go back that way." The boy took the ball and splashed his way back to his dad.

Razor smiled as he imagined Eve with her own little boy. Family. He wouldn't mind having a family someday. He wouldn't mind having a family with Eve.

"Zack! What's with the goofy grin?"

"Nothing. I was pissing in the ocean."

She slapped his arm in a playful way. "Does anyone else know what a sense of humor you have?"

Shrugging, he didn't say anything as they went back to their things, and he drank a bottle of water. They reclined on the beach towels and soaked up the sun. It was a beautiful day, not a cloud in the sky.

"Zack?"

"Yeah?"

"Where are you going to live?" Eve asked.

He was a little surprised by the question. "Uh, I'm going to live with my parents until I figure something out. I'm thinking of getting a mobile home and living on the property so that I'll be close. Why?"

"Just curious," Eve said.

Razor adjusted his sunglasses and looked at her. *She wouldn't like the country. Would she? Cows, dirt, and cow shit. No, she's too classy for that.* He closed his eyes and turned his head back toward the sky.

It didn't take long for the heat to take its toll. Razor sat up and looked at Eve in her bikini.

"Are you staring at me?"

"Yes. You're beautiful."

Eve smiled. "I'm hot."

"Yes, you are," he said.

"No, I meant that I'm going back in the water." She stood up and waited for Razor. "Are you coming?"

"Yeah." He rose and followed her back into the ocean. They swam out to a depth that covered Eve's shoulders. Razor pulled her close and kissed her. He slowly backed into deeper water and held her when she couldn't touch the bottom. Eve had her arms around his neck, holding on. Then Razor took a free hand and pulled the string around her neck.

"What are you doing?"

He was silent as the strings around her neck fell into the ocean. Razor took a finger and placed it gently on her lips and slowly moved it down her chin, her neck, and stopped briefly at her clavicle. Continuing the path, he went down her cleavage and decided to move his right hand to her left breast, cupping it.

"Zack," she whispered as he began to tease her nipple with his thumb. He smiled as it hardened and stood erect.

"Let yourself go, Eve," he said kissing her neck. He moved his hand down into her bikini bottom and began teasing her with his fingers.

Eve couldn't help but moan as she wrapped her legs around him, but gave him enough space so his fingers could continue their quest. Her eyes were closed as she held on to his neck and moaned again. No one was near them and all she heard were the sounds of the water lapping against them. She could smell the brine of the salt water on his skin with each inhalation. As he worked his magic, Eve's breathing became short and fast until he felt her squeeze his neck hard and he knew his mission was successful. She relaxed and let her legs drop from around him.

"You are terrible, Zachary Reston."

"You didn't like that? Seemed to me you enjoyed it."

"I didn't say I didn't enjoy it." She grabbed him and felt how hard he was. Smiling, she swam away and then tied her bikini top around her neck.

"Eve. Hey, are you going to leave me here?" he called after her.

Knowing he wouldn't leave the water with an erection she stopped and turned to look at him. The look on his face was one of disbelief. Eve swam back out to him.

"Come on, honey. Fair is fair."

"Are you sure?"

"Whales do it out here. Dolphins."

She wrinkled her nose. "Thanks for that visual. Now when I look out my balcony I'll be thinking of all the creatures in the ocean screwing around."

"I was hoping you'd think of me." His face dropped in sadness.

"Oh my gosh. Stop that. Puppy dog eyes." She swam closer and he held her. "You're unbelievable."

He grabbed her hand and stopped her from touching him. "I'm messing with you. You don't have to do that. Letting me satisfy you was enough." He gave her a kiss and then picked her up and tossed her away.

"Zack!" Eve yelled when she came up from the water. She looked around and saw him swimming farther out into the ocean. "Silly frogman." Knowing he couldn't hear her she admitted, "I'm really going to miss you." Eve began swimming back toward the shore.

*****

Eve noticed the sudden darkness over her as if a cloud had passed over the sun. Then she felt the drops of water. Opening her eyes, she saw a dark figure standing over her. "You're dripping on me."

Ignoring her comment, Razor said, "I'm getting hungry."

"Me too. Let's go back and get cleaned up for lunch." Eve stood up after taking his hand. She glanced down at the scar on his right side. Touching it gently, she said, "It healed nicely."

He grunted and gave her a quick kiss. They picked up their things and returned to the condo. After taking a shower and changing into clean clothes, they went downstairs to Eve's SUV. She handed him the key fob again. Razor drove to a nearby casual restaurant on the beach, and they sat outside. Halfway through the meal, Razor said, "You know, I wouldn't say no if you wanted to come for a visit."

Eve didn't hesitate. "I'd like that. I'll look at my schedule and see when I can take some time off."

They finished their meal, and Razor drove back to the condo. He went inside and picked up his things. She walked him to the door, and he said, "Eve."

"I know. You're going." She sniffed as her eyes began to water. She swallowed and kissed him one last time. "I'll miss you, Razor."

"Call me Zack. I like it when you call me Zack," he told her.

"I'll miss you, Zack," she said, hugging him tightly.

"I'll miss you, Eve."

In all their time together, they never said they loved each other. They both felt it but never said it out loud. They let go of each other, and he opened the door and walked into the hall.

"Zack! I love you!" she called.

He paused but didn't turn around. Then he began walking again. "I love you too," he said quietly.

CHAPTER 7

The driving time was about twenty-two hours. Razor stopped and spent the night at a hotel that day and then got up early and drove through to his parents' place about twenty minutes from the town of Willis, Texas. Turning onto a dirt and gravel road, he opened the gate, drove through, and closed it again. Getting back in the truck, he grabbed his phone from the center console and pulled up Eve's name to send her a short text: Arrived safely. He slowly drove the short distance to the house, where he was met by barking dogs. His phone dinged, and he read the reply: Glad to hear it. It was followed by a heart emoji. He smiled and got out of the truck as his mother came out and shooed the dogs away. His father followed slowly behind her.

"Zack! So good to see you, son," his mother said, hugging him.

"Hi, Mom. Good to be here."

"Zack." His father held out his hand.

"Dad." Razor noticed that his father looked tired and frail since the last time he saw him. His handshake was also weaker than he remembered. His sister was right in what she'd told him about his health.

"I'm glad you're here, son. You can stay in your old room until you find a place," his father said. Like Razor, his father was also a man of few words, saying only what was necessary. He turned and went back inside the house.

"Are you hungry, son?" his mother asked as they walked up the steps and into the home his father had built more than forty years ago.

"No, just tired of driving."

"Get some sleep. We need to check the fence in the morning," his father said.

"Yes, sir," Razor said as he went to put his things in his old room.

*****

A few days later, Razor went to look at mobile homes. He purchased a small one and had it placed on the property. That gave him the independence he needed while staying close. He worked hard on the small parcel of land, mending fences, feeding the herd, and chasing down the occasional escaped cow. He hated those cows, but it gave his parents an agricultural exemption on their taxes. The house was old and also needed some repairing. He found he enjoyed spending time with his parents. He'd often take his mom to the grocery store just to spend some time alone with her.

Kimberly A. Biggerstaff © 2025

One morning at breakfast, his mother asked, "Zack, would you like to go to the American Legion post with us? It's bingo night, but they have a bar if you don't want to play. You can talk to other veterans." It was the first time his mother had asked him to go. She was starting to have trouble driving at night, and his father had stopped driving after he ran over one of the dogs.

"Sure, Mom." He took them to the post and hung out in the bar while they played bingo. A few people said hello, but he didn't really engage. His mother got him when they were ready to leave.

"Did you have fun, Zack?" his mother asked from the back seat of his truck on the way home.

"It was fine. How about you? Win any money?"

"Ten dollars."

"Better than nothing. Dad, did you enjoy it?"

"Think I'd rather hang out with you at the bar," his father said.

"Ray, you're just mad that you didn't win anything this time."

Zack laughed. "You're welcome to hang out with me."

"Did you join?" Ray asked.

"Join what?" Zack asked.

"The American Legion, son. The post," Ray said.

"Uh, no."

His father sighed. "I'll sign you up. Do you know what we do? It's more than just bingo and a canteen. Have you ever heard of the American Legion? They're a Veterans Service Organization—VSO. We help vets and their families. If you want to keep your veteran benefits, you need to join. Your mother and I are members."

"Mom's not a vet."

"The auxiliary, Zack. That's what I'm a member of," his mother explained.

"Martha and the others do their own thing to help vets and families," Ray told him.

"OK, Dad. Sign me up," Zack told him. "You can still join me for a beer."

The following week Ray signed Zack up for membership in the American Legion. He wasn't sure he'd go to meetings, but he offered to help in other ways. He volunteered to help build a ramp at the home of a veteran who used a wheelchair and to cut the grass at the home of another one. He was happy to assist other service members, and his mother was glad he was getting out.

Ray was sitting at the bar with Zack when he said, "My heart isn't good."

"What? You're a good man, Dad."

"No, physically. You need to look after your mother. The fellows here will do my funeral. It's in my will."

"Dad. You've got plenty of years left." Then he added, "Yes, I'll look after mom."

That was all Ray wanted to say on the subject. "Got a girl?" he asked.

"Sort of. It's complicated now that I'm here." Zack still thought about Eve every now and then, but he'd been so busy, he hadn't contacted her but once other than the time he'd arrived here.

*****

A week later his mother called him while he was out buying feed for the cows. "Yeah, Mom?"

"Zachary, you need to come home. It's your father."

Razor knew something serious was wrong. He heard it in her voice. He closed the tailgate on his truck and got home as quickly as he could. His father was sitting in his chair in front of the TV. He looked as if he was sleeping, but Razor checked his pulse. He was gone. He'd fallen asleep in front of the television and hadn't woken up. For some reason, it didn't surprise Razor. They'd learn later that he'd had a heart attack.

He thought back to the conversation he'd had with his father at the post. *I'll take care of Mom and everything, Dad.* He looked at his mother. "Are you OK, Mom?" He walked to her, and she fell into his arms and began to cry.

*****

Kimberly A. Biggerstaff © 2025

Razor called his sister, Lori, and brother, Danny, who came for the funeral and spent some time with their mother. Razor had taken care of everything, including the funeral arrangements. His mother reminded Razor to call the American Legion post and ask if they had an honor guard or something that could come out for the burial. They laid his father to rest in the Houston VA National Cemetery. His mother asked him to wear his uniform.

Razor had been staying in his old room in the house in case his mother needed anything. He pulled his navy-blue dress uniform out of the closet and hung it on the back of a door. Looking it over, he made sure everything was perfect. He'd done it last night, but he checked it again. Medals, ribbons, insignias, devices. Everything was straight, neat, and clean. Putting on his uniform, he walked outside to the twenty-five-foot flagpole and brought the American flag down and then raised it back to half-staff. Securing it, Razor took a step back and saluted in a slow manner. "For you, Dad. Fair winds and following seas."

*****

"Your father was proud of you, Zack," Martha told him at the funeral. "Proud of your service. He loved seeing the photos of you in your uniform."

Razor couldn't say anything. He was quiet as they got through the funeral and drove to the cemetery. Sitting by his mother, he held her hand during the graveside ceremony. When it was time, the funeral director asked everyone to rise for the rendering of honors. The post honor guard, who had been waiting at parade rest nearby, snapped to attention, and seven members fired three volleys of rounds. Razor delivered a crisp salute as taps played.

Razor had been to a few of these over the years. Fallen friends who died in service to their country. Fellow SEALs he knew and respected. One navy friend had committed suicide. That one was difficult because his buddy didn't leave a note, and there were so many unanswered questions. No one had seen any signs that he'd been thinking about ending his life.

Everyone resumed their seats as two active duty navy members folded the flag. Razor had gone to the local recruiter's office and asked if he would help at the ceremony by folding the flag. He had even arrived in uniform, hoping it would mean more and that the recruiter would agree. Razor had told him that it was the same recruiting office he'd come to twenty-one years before. The recruiter had said that he'd be honored to assist and that he'd contact another active duty friend to help.

So, there they were, folding the flag slowly and neatly. It was passed to the detail leader, who knelt in front of Razor's mother and, holding the flag in his white-gloved hands, said, "On behalf of the president of the United States, the United

States Navy, and a grateful nation, please accept this flag as a symbol of our appreciation for your loved one's honorable and faithful service." The man stood and gave a slow salute. He offered his condolences to Razor and his brother and sister. Then he marched with the others to wait for everyone to begin leaving. Razor made a point to go over and thank the recruiter, his friend, and the honor guard from the post for their service and for assisting in his father's funeral. Razor invited everyone back to the post for a reception and refreshments.

"You did a great job with everything, Zack. Thank you," Danny said. "If there's anything we can do for the next couple of days, let us know."

"Sure." But Razor knew they were hollow words from his older brother. He meant well but wasn't very responsible. It was all he could do to meet his alimony and child support payments. Razor knew Danny needed to get back home to Grapevine, Texas, and return to work.

His sister, Lori, offered to stay for another week and be with his mother. Her husband and the two kids had to get back to work and school. Lori helped Martha pack some of their father's clothes to donate, and they went through mementos and his things.

At the end of the week, Razor thanked Lori and told her he'd be in touch if something came up.

*****

Razor knew he needed to keep his mother busy. He took her shopping and to any appointments she had. Keeping up with the cows and the dogs, mending the fence, and making repairs on the house were beginning to take a toll on him. He was getting tired, and the nightmares had started up again. The stress of it all was wearing him down. The things he'd done and seen as a SEAL came back to haunt him when he slept. Remembering the time he caught a round in his side. The time Cobra got hurt, holding his hand and telling him he would be OK. Watching the life drain from his eyes. Pounding the trident pin into his coffin. His hand turning to a fist and pounding it again and again. Running toward a helicopter ready to take them to safety. Firing his weapon at the enemy. The enemy, some hiding in plain sight. Gathering intelligence, destroying tunnels. Disjointed flashes of missions filled his nightmares.

He'd wake up sweating and then couldn't go back to sleep. Razor kept his weapon under his pillow for self-defense in the mobile home. Sometimes he'd find himself awake, pointing his weapon at an imaginary enemy.

Razor still took his mother to the post for bingo, but he started drinking more every time they went. He was building up a tolerance. One night he crossed the yellow line while driving, and his mother yelled at him. When they arrived home, Razor promised her that it wouldn't happen again. He kept his promise when he drove her anywhere. At home and anywhere else was a different story. He was drinking a lot in his mobile home. He slept late, and some days he wouldn't go see his mother. Every day was the same. Wake up, do chores, go to bed, have a nightmare, repeat, with a lot of drinking in between. He had hoped the drinking would stop the nightmares, but it didn't. One night his sister, Lori, called him.

Lori was a couple of years older than Zack. She lived in Athens, Texas, about two hours and twenty minutes away. She worked full time while taking care of her family. She kept in touch with Martha and called more often since her father passed away. But Martha had called her and said she was worried about Razor.

"Are you all right, Zack?" Lori asked when he finally answered the phone.

"No. You need to take Mom so that I can sell this fucking hellhole." He hung up.

Two days later, Lori showed up and knocked on the door to his mobile home. He was drunk. "What's going on, Zack?" Lori asked.

"I'm tired. Leave me alone."

"Mom won't leave, Zack," his sister told him.

"I know."

"You need to clean up and talk to her. She listens to you."

"Fine. Go away," Razor said, slamming the door.

Razor took a shower and drank three cups of coffee. He needed to eat something, but the bread was beginning to get moldy, and he hadn't been to the grocery store in two weeks. He dug around in a backpack and found a protein bar. He ate it and drank a glass of tap water. Taking a deep breath, Razor walked to his mother's house. Lori was folding some laundry and didn't say anything to him. He headed to the kitchen, where he found his mother putting dishes away.

"Are you hungry?" Martha asked.

"Yes, ma'am."

"Go feed the cows and come back."

"Yes, ma'am."

His mother handed him a bottle of Gatorade. Razor took it and left.

*****

Lori stayed for a few days, presumably hoping Razor would come to his senses. But she didn't know how bad it was getting. The nightmares were happening nightly now. He would wake up sweating and disoriented. But he convinced Lori to go back home to her family. She didn't understand anyway.

Before she left, she spoke to him privately. "Zack, I tried to talk to Mom about getting rid of the cows. I even suggested just selling a few for now, but she's not ready. Maybe you could talk to her."

*****

The next morning, Razor took a shower and cleaned up. He walked to his mother's and asked if she had time to talk.

"Yes, Zack. What is it?" She was washing dishes.

"Mom, would you sit, please?"

"I'm listening. Go ahead. By the way, the water isn't flowing like it should."

Razor sighed. *"Mom!"*

"Don't raise your voice to me, young man." She turned and stared at him. That stare. It was probably where he got it.

"I'm sorry. Look, this house is old, and the cows are too much. We need to think about making some changes. Lori said you could live with her."

"No. I'm not leaving. Hire a teenager to help you. Or maybe a veteran."

"You don't have the money to . . ." He stopped talking because he knew it was no use. She wasn't ready to leave. He turned and walked out to get some tools to fix the sink.

*****

Razor sobered up for a few weeks, although he still had nightmares. It didn't last long, and he began drinking again. He was tired from the lack of sleep, and he'd lost some weight. His temper was short, and he snapped at his mother more than once. She slapped him after the last time.

Kimberly A. Biggerstaff © 2025

"I'm still your mother, and you will not treat me like that," she told him. "Your father would be disappointed in you, Zachary."

What his mother said hurt him more than the slap. He went back to his mobile home and drank a bottle of whiskey until he passed out. When he woke, he saw his Sig Sauer P365-XL sitting on the table. He picked it up and went outside. It was dark. He stood in the grass with the weapon in one hand, wearing nothing but his boxer shorts. Taking a breath, he reached down with his free hand and took a piss. He closed his eyes while the stream continued. Suddenly, he heard a noise and opened his eyes to find the bull standing nearby, staring at him. Razor raised the handgun at it.

"Son of a bitch," he said as he felt the liquid hit his foot. "I should shoot you right now, you motherfucker." He sighed. "Is there a hole in the fence, or did you jump it?" Razor turned to go inside but looked back at the bull. "Don't shit here. This is my territory. Go away." Razor took a quick shower, then went to bed. He thought about the ocean and how different his life was. He hated it here. He'd spent too much time in the Norfolk and Virginia Beach area. He loved it there. *The water, the surf, the beach, Eve in a bikini . . .* He shook his head to try to get her out of his thoughts. It had been too long, and she was probably busy with work, if she hadn't moved on. She had texted him twice, but he never responded. Long-distance relationships are hard. *You promised Dad you'd take care of Mom. You can't let him down again.* There were times when Razor thought about texting Eve, but then he had to fix something, or feed the stupid cows, or chase down that damn bull. He'd get distracted and forget. The more time that passed, the less he thought about her. *She's better off,* he thought as he went to the fridge, grabbed a beer, and swallowed the contents quickly. Going back to bed, he tried to think about the waves of the ocean as sleep eluded him.

*****

The next morning he rode the ATV around the property line to check for holes in the fence. Finding one, he went back, put the supplies in his truck, and headed back to fix it. Razor was tired and grumpy. Mumbling to himself about how much he hated the cows, he went to get a hammer and stepped in a big cow patty. "Shit!" Looking at the culprit, he walked over and punched it in its rear haunch, chasing it away. Going to the back of the truck, he slammed the tailgate shut, climbed inside, and saw a bottle of whiskey on the floor. Picking it up, he downed as much as he could. Wiping his mouth, he drove back to his mobile home and drank the rest of the bottle.

*****

Feeling a sense of déjà vu, Razor woke up, grabbed his gun, and stared at it. The weapon felt good in his hand. He missed going to the range and shooting. Staying drunk all day made going to the range out of the question. He wasn't that stupid. No, he'd leave his stupidity for home. Again, he went outside to take a piss. Looking around for that damn bull, he instead pointed the handgun at a cow on the other side of the fence. It was resting in the grass and dirt. Razor sat on the steps of the mobile home. It was getting cool at night, but even sitting there in his boxers, he was hot and still a little drunk. He stared at the gun in his hand. *How many lives over the years had he taken with weapons like this? The enemy. Who was the enemy now? There was no enemy. Just cows. Fucking cows and yourself. You're letting them down, Reston. Mom and Dad. Is it worth it?* He snorted and went back inside.

At ten the next morning, Martha called him. Waking up on his couch with the gun on his chest, it fell to the floor as he sat up. Razor looked around for his phone. His place was a mess. Empty bottles, plates, bowls, and mail were all over the tables and floor. Finally finding his phone, he answered it.

"Yeah?"

"I need to go to the grocery store, Zack," Martha told him.

Running a hand over his head, he said, "I'll be there in twenty minutes or so." Razor showered and dressed, then drove to his mother's. She was sitting in a rocking chair on the porch waiting for him. Walking down to the truck, she waited by the passenger door. Razor quickly got out to open it for her.

"Manners, Zachary."

He knew better, but he was tired and worn out. He didn't say anything to her as they drove to the grocery store twenty minutes away. Razor helped get everything she needed and picked up some things for himself. His mother gave him a look as he bought a case of beer, but he ignored her. On the way home, his mother received a call.

When she hung up, she said, "The bull is two properties down."

Razor held in what he wanted to say and instead cursed in his head. He growled. "I'll get it." Arriving home, he helped put the groceries away, then made a sandwich and grabbed a Gatorade. "Which way?" he asked his mother.

"North."

He changed out of his nice jeans and boots and put on his work ones. He found a rope and headed north. His tracking skills came in handy as he walked along looking for the bull. He saw it on the property of the family who had called his mother. Jumping a fence, he closed in on it, but it snorted and took off. "Bastard." Razor followed him into some brush and spooked him. He tried to steer him back toward their property, but it was difficult. After two hours, Razor was hot, sweaty, and very pissed off. The bull was too.

Chasing him to an open area, Razor swung the lasso and threw it but missed. It wasn't the first time he'd missed. It had been a while since he'd had to lasso an animal. On deployments he lassoed a couple of goats. A few times he even lassoed his buddies when they were killing time.

"All right, you son of a bitch. Let's go." Razor swung the lasso over his head, determined to best the beast. The black bull snorted at him in defiance. He was as tired of this game as Razor was. Like the bulls in the rings of Spain or Mexico, he charged the body in front of him.

Razor stood his ground and moved as he approached. As the bull passed him, he threw the lasso; it landed on the bull's neck. "Gotcha!" Razor said, holding the rope and running after him. The bull stopped, giving up. Razor leaned over and whispered in his ear. "Listen here, you fucker. I'm tired of this shit. If you don't start acting right, I'm going to gut you, real slow. Understand?" He knew his words meant nothing to this creature, but he felt a little better saying them. Besides, he would never torture an animal. Razor smacked him on his rear to get him to walk as he led the bull back home.

"Finally got him," a woman called. The best way back was to go to the road and then cut down a path to a back gate and release the bull onto their property.

"Yes, ma'am. You want him?" Razor asked.

"No. But my husband might be interested in some of the cows or the property someday. I was sorry to hear about your father. Nice man."

"Thanks. Mom's not ready, but I'll keep it in mind."

"Good luck," she said, turning her attention back to the little boy throwing mud at his sister. "Johnny!"

*****

After letting the bull back on the property, Razor walked to his mother's house and told her he had captured the animals.

"Good. Now go shower and change. It's bingo night."

Razor's sense of accomplishment was suddenly gone. "Fuck bingo night!" As soon as the words left his mouth, he regretted saying it. "I'm sorry, Mom."

But she was already gone. She walked back to her bedroom and slammed the door. He growled and returned to his mobile home. He took off his shirt and boots, then grabbed a beer. He downed it and searched for something stronger. "Fuck!" he yelled when he couldn't find any whiskey. He grabbed the closest T-shirt and put it on, along with his boots. Razor drove to the nearest liquor store and bought three bottles of whiskey, then returned to the back gate of the property and began drinking. When it started getting dark, Razor pulled his handgun from the glove box, then climbed into the bed of his truck with the whiskey bottle. Leaning against the back window, he took a swig. He looked up at the stars. "I get it now, Travis," he whispered as his eyes watered. Travis was his navy buddy who had taken his own life. Razor took another swig, then another.

CHAPTER 8

The sun beating down on his face woke him. Razor pushed himself up and knocked the nearly empty whiskey bottle so that it clattered across the bed of the truck. "Shut up!" he said, holding his head. His mouth was dry, and his head was pounding. He reached for the bottle and took a gulp from it. *Hair of the dog.* But his stomach couldn't handle it, and he leaned over and threw up over the side. "What are you looking at, bastard?" he said to the bull, who was staring at him. His phone was nearby. As he focused on it, he saw the text messages he'd sent. "Shit." They were all to Eve. His phone was hot from spending the morning hours in the sun and shut off before he could read them. Climbing down from the bed of the truck, he looked around and did his business. He glanced at the bull, who also took a piss. "I'm tired of your shit. If you're not careful, I'll shoot you and eat your heart," he said. "You've been warned, twice."

Getting into the truck, Razor drove to his mobile home. He charged his phone and took a shower. He toweled off, not even bothering to dress, then made some toast and drank a large bottle of Gatorade. He grabbed a handful of sliced deli meat and shoved it in his mouth. Razor walked to the bedroom, pulled the towel from his waist, and put on a pair of clean boxers. He heard his phone ding and make multiple noises. Taking some aspirin, he grabbed the phone and the charging cord and sat on the couch. He plugged it in again and read the texts he sent to Eve. I hate my life. I miss you. I made a mistake. Forget what I said. Move on with your life. I'm no good. Have a nice life. Everyone's better off without me. Fuck you and this life! Goodbye!

He had sent her ten texts. He checked the call log. One incoming call from Eve. But no message. He didn't remember it. He didn't remember anything except yelling at his mother. Taking a deep breath, he texted his mother to apologize. Razor knew the text wouldn't be enough, though. An hour later he was standing in her kitchen, feeling like he did when he was fifteen and got caught drinking with some boys from school.

"I'm sorry for what I said to you, Mom. You didn't deserve that. I'll take you to the next bingo night."

"Apology accepted. Is that your laundry?" she asked, seeing the green military duffel bag on his shoulder.

"Yes, ma'am."

"Give it here."

"I can do it."

"No. You have other chores. Start with the garbage."

"Yes, ma'am," he said.

*****

For a few days, things were fine. He stayed sober but wasn't happy. The next time he went to the feed store, they told him his chickens had arrived. "What chickens?" Evidently, his father had ordered some chickens, and the coop was on layaway with one payment left. "Well, we won't have to buy eggs," he said, paying for everything and loading up his truck.

Martha didn't know about the chickens but said they'd give it a go. Razor built the coop but had to go back and buy fencing to keep the dogs and any other animals away.

The added chore meant more stress, and it was beginning to build up again. Razor took his mother to bingo, like he promised, but sat in the bar and drank. He also consumed a lot of water to slow himself down so that he could drive home. After dropping his mom off, he decided he didn't want to go home. He found a bar he'd never been to and continued drinking.

*****

Groaning, Razor looked at his watch. It was four in the morning. *Where the fuck am I?* he wondered as he looked around. He glanced at the naked woman beside him. She was on her stomach and had some tattoos on her back and arms. She stirred and turned over.

Getting up, she went to the bathroom. Razor just sat there. *Shit.* Trying to get his bearings, he looked around for his clothes.

"Hey, baby." The woman came back and smiled at him, then went to the nightstand and snorted a line of coke. She handed him the rolled-up bill. "Your turn."

"What? No fucking way."

"Oh, right. You enjoyed it this way." She grabbed a small envelope from the table and lay next to him. He watched as she carefully poured some of the white powder between her breasts. "Go ahead."

"No."

"Don't waste it, baby. Come on. Do it, and then we'll have some fun. You were an animal last night." The woman went to grab his manhood, but Razor pushed her hand away.

He got up and found his clothes. Checking his wallet to make sure his money and credit cards were still there, he walked out of the trailer. *Where the hell am I?* Locating his truck, Razor drove away from the trailer park. Down the road, he pulled over to find out where he was by using the map app on his phone. He returned home, cursing himself the entire way.

In his driveway, he turned off the truck and sat there. He reached in his glove box for his handgun, but it wasn't there. "Shit!" Feeling around the floorboard, he breathed a sigh of relief when he found it under his seat. Staring at it, Razor felt lost. All his emotions came to the surface, and his eyes welled up. He was tired, lost, angry, depressed, sad, and lonely. Lifting the gun, he placed it on his temple. His trigger discipline kept his finger along the side of the weapon and not on the trigger itself. His hand was shaking slightly. He closed his eyes and took a deep breath. Hearing a noise, he opened his eyes. For a brief moment, he thought he saw Eve's face. Wiping the tears away, the image morphed into the bull. It stared at him through the window. Razor laughed and climbed out of the truck. "Why do you keep tormenting me?" He stood in the darkness and looked at the sky. Taking a breath, he walked up the steps to his home and went inside.

Razor was disgusted with himself. He stripped off his clothes and took a hot shower, praying he wasn't so stupid as to not protect himself. After sufficiently sanitizing his skin, he double-checked his wallet. No condoms, good. *This is a new low. Drugs? Really?* Pulling his boxers on, he went back to bed and took a nap.

*****

About seven o'clock, he fixed some coffee and walked down to his mother's. Martha was cooking some eggs and bacon, and when she heard him, she fixed more.

"Don't forget about the chickens," she told him.

"Yes, ma'am."

*****

Razor worked hard that day and the following ones. But he was still having nightmares and drinking in the evenings. He'd drive to the post around five and sit at the bar and drink until it was late, not talking to anyone. Some mornings, he wondered how he made it home. A few more times, he woke up in his truck. He was miserable.

He sat in his truck one night and looked at his handgun. "Just do it. The nightmares will end, and it'll be easier for everyone. Danny and Lori can take care of Mom." He placed the gun under his chin. Then against his temple. Then, with tears running down his cheeks, he began to laugh. He set the gun down on the seat. "Chickenshit!" Razor screamed as he gripped the steering wheel with all his might. His knuckles turned white as his voice finally cracked. He looked at the beer bottles and cans on the floor of the truck. There was a whiskey bottle next to his weapon. Razor picked up his phone and stared at it. He pulled up Eve's name. His thumb hovered above the phone symbol. When the screen timed out and went dark he grabbed the gun and went inside his home.

*****

CHAPTER 9

Two days later, at the post, a man sat next to Razor and asked, "Reston, isn't it?"

"What?"

"You're Zack Reston, right? Helped out a bit before your dad passed?" the man asked. He was a longtime member of the American Legion and a volunteer.

"Yeah, that's me," Razor said, taking a sip of his beer.

"Did you bring your mother for bingo?"

Razor sighed. He wasn't in the mood to talk. "Yeah."

"Good. I was army. What branch were you?"

"Navy frogman. Call me Razor," he said.

"Tim over there was navy." He pointed to an older gentleman at a table with a woman. "Hey, Tim! What were you in the navy?"

"Seabees," Tim said.

"Got a frogman here."

"About time we got one of those. Welcome aboard, kid."

"Kid?" Razor said. A year under forty, he didn't consider himself a kid. But as he looked around, he noticed most of the men and women in the post were older. There were a few who were younger. One had on a shirt on that read SONS OF THE AMERICAN LEGION.

"I'm Jack," he said. He sat by Razor for another hour. They didn't say much. Razor kept drinking while trying to ignore him. "Your mother asked me to speak to you. She's worried about you and thought you might want to talk to another man."

"I'm handling it," he lied, then picked up the glass of water and took a big gulp.

Jack seemed to be able to tell that something was wrong and finally asked, "Razor, have you ever wished you were dead?"

Razor looked at his beer, staying silent. He was surprised that Jack just came right out and asked him that. He began to pick at the label on his beer bottle. *Why should I talk to this guy? I don't know him. Why talk to anyone? Nothing will change. The cows, chickens, and chores will still be there. I can't do this anymore.* The lump in his throat grew. *Screw it. The old man wants to hear me bitch about my life, fine.* Before Jack could ask his next question, Razor said, "Moving back has been tough. I was prepared to help out, but it turned out to be more than I expected." He took a swig of his beer. "I'm having nightmares from my service time. We saw some bad shit."

"Got a few guys here with PTSD. Been to the VA?"

"No. Been taking care of the farm. Fucking cows get out, have to chase them down, fix the fence, feed the cows, fix the house. Dad ordered chickens before he died. Another thing to take care of. I hate it. Never should have left the beach."

"Why did you?"

"Had to take care of Mom and Dad. Now just Mom. Promised Dad." He paused and finally answered Jack's original question about wishing he were dead. "Yeah, I thought about it. It'd be easy, just pull the trigger. Right there in my truck. Check out. Let my brother and sister deal with the shit." He took a gulp of his beer. "Big, tough Navy SEAL turned chickenshit and couldn't pull the trigger. I'm a fucking whiner."

Razor couldn't believe he'd just said all that and admitted he thought about killing himself.

"You're not whining or complaining. It's tough leaving the service for some of us. Especially if you've been in combat. I won't pretend to know what you've seen or done, but I was in Nam. Just a grunt, but those patrols were hell. It was hard when I came back. Especially because so many protested the war. I never would have worn a hat like this back then." Razor glanced at his ball cap. Embroidered on it was VIETNAM VETERAN, along with the National Defense Service ribbon, the Vietnam Service ribbon, and the RVN Vietnam Campaign ribbon.

"Yeah, I heard you guys were treated like shit. Sorry," Razor said.

"Thanks. Back to you. I'd like to help you, son. Help a fellow vet. Will you let me?" Jack asked.

"No." Razor didn't want any help. He just wanted to sit and drink. He was already regretting what he'd told Jack.

Jack crossed his arms on the stool and ordered a Dr Pepper. "I can't leave you. I'm not going to let you leave here by yourself. I asked one of the ladies to take your mother home. We can sit here until closing."

Razor took a drink and began to mull over his options. Maybe he should talk to his mother about downsizing again. Start with that bull. Thirty minutes passed and Razor finally said, "I miss her."

"What's that, son?"

"I miss her. Eve," Razor said.

"Was that your girl?" Jack asked.

"Sort of. I guess. Sometimes."

"Call her."

"No." Razor thought about everything. He had texted her while he was drunk and was not exactly nice. "I'm sure she's moved on by now." For some reason, Cobra entered his mind. They were ambushed and took fire. Cobra was hit badly, but Razor stayed with him. Razor was trying to treat his wound when Cobra saw an enemy combatant sneak up behind Razor.

With all the energy he had left, Cobra raised his weapon and fired at the enemy, saving Razor's life. "Fair winds . . . and following . . . seas," Cobra gasped with his last breath. Razor insisted on getting him to the exfil point. When it was safe and time to go, Razor used the fireman's carry to bring him out.

In the debrief Razor told them what Cobra did and suggested a medal. Cobra received his medal posthumously, and Razor was left with survivor's guilt, which didn't rear its ugly head until later. It should have been him. He'd be dead if Cobra hadn't killed the man. Suddenly, he was overwhelmed with emotions. A tear landed on the bar as he looked down. Jack placed a comforting hand on his back for a moment. It was then that Razor knew he couldn't go on like this anymore.

"It's more than the farm and missing your girl, isn't it?" Jack asked rhetorically. "You need to get help, son. Let me take you to get that help." Razor nodded, and Jack patted his back. "I'll go with you, Razor. Whenever you're ready."

*****

Jack drove Razor to the hospital and then called Martha. "Mrs. Reston?"

"Yes."

"This is Jack Crane from the Legion post."

"Oh my god, is it Zachary? Is he—"

"He's at the hospital, ma'am. He's not hurt, and he's safe."

"Did he get in an accident?"

"No, ma'am. He's at Michael DeBakey VA Hospital in Houston. He's been having some issues and thoughts of suicide."

"Oh my God. Did he try something?"

"He's safe, ma'am. Here, you can talk to him." Jack handed Razor the phone.

"Mom? I'm sorry. For everything. I need to take some time and get myself sorted out. I'm safe," he told her in a soft voice.

"Zachary. I love you, son," Martha said as she began to cry silently.

"I need some time, Mom."

"Take all the time you need, son. Please, just get better and let me know if I can help you. I'll call you tomorrow morning."

"Thanks, Mom."

*****

Talking about his feelings was difficult for Razor. If anything, he preferred the individual sessions instead of the group therapy. Sharing his emotions with a bunch of strangers just wasn't in his character. Opening up to Jack was an anomaly. Razor was the strong, silent type. But he listened to the other veterans tell their stories. He knew he wasn't alone and hearing what the others had to say did help, but he was better one-on-one.

*****

One month later, Razor found he'd been sleeping better since he'd been going to therapy. He was sound asleep when his phone rang. He reached for his phone and answered as quickly as he could without looking at his caller ID.

"Yeah?"

Samantha Barrett wasn't sure she wanted to talk to him now. She was feeling down and wanted to call her psychiatrist, but it was too early, and his office wasn't open yet. She tried to call another friend, Hammer, but it went to voicemail. Razor was the next person she'd thought of.

"Hello?" He waited. He'd been through this before. Guys calling him. Buddies on the brink of life or death. For the past week Razor had been checking in with his old friends and teammates to make sure they were OK. He didn't want anyone to go through what he'd been through. Something he'd learned from therapy was that his personality made him keep things inside. One of his outlets, combat missions, was gone now. "It's OK. I can wait until you're ready. Just don't do anything. I'll wait."

Finally, Sam spoke. "Is this a suicide hotline you're working, Razor?"

"Who is this?" Women rarely called him.

"I still have your knife."

Razor smiled. "Barrett. How are you? Need some help with a mission? I freelance now."

"Most of you guys do. No. It's just too early to call my doctor."

"But it's not too early to call me? All right, what's wrong?" Razor asked, concerned about his old friend.

"Just life. It kind of sucks."

"Yeah, that happens. Have you had thoughts of killing yourself?"

"No. I mean, yeah, but not now. I've already been through that. Why did you go there?" Sam asked.

"I've lost some buddies to suicide. After I retired, I joined an American Legion post. You heard of them?"

"Of course. They're a Veterans Service Organization. They help veterans and their families."

"Yeah. I originally went just because they had a bar. I took my mother to bingo. I was having trouble transitioning to civilian life and taking care of my parents' farm was stressful. I was drinking a lot and hit rock bottom. Woke up a few times in my truck with my gun in my hand."

"Razor," she said quietly, letting him tell his story.

"Anyway, one of the older guys started talking to me. Then he listened. Stayed with me and got me help. They have a program called Be the One. Be the one to save a veteran's life.

Saving lives and changing lives. If that guy hadn't talked to me, I wouldn't be here. After I got better, I wanted to pay it back. They have this training to recognize those who might need help. I took the training and try to help fellow vets."

"That's commendable, Razor. Inspiring."

"Why did you call, Star girl? Just to shoot the shit? Want to have a beer?"

"Unless you're in Ireland—it's a long way for a beer run."

"Yeah, that's a little far. Work or pleasure?" Razor asked.

"I needed to get away."

"Have you done anything, started to do anything, or prepared to do anything to end your life?"

"What are you doing? Reading from a card?"

"It's the Columbia Protocol. Answer the questions."

"No. I have a doctor I talk to once or twice a week."

"OK. You're low risk."

"I appreciate what you're doing. I just needed to hear . . . look, I don't have many friends. I miss my baby daughter. I got mad at John—"

"John? John who?"

"Burke," Sam said.

Razor smiled. He knew how his friend John Burke felt about Sam. He'd told Razor to watch her back on that mission in Sweden years before. "Little John? Are you with him?"

"We have a son, Jonathan. He's fifteen. Nearly sixteen," Sam answered.

"Really? That's great. Wait, you have a baby daughter too? Not John's?"

"It's a long story. I made a mistake, got mad, and told John to take everyone and leave. He did. But they stayed away. They weren't supposed to stay away."

"Want me to kick Little John's ass?" Razor offered.

"Yes. Would you?" Sam said. She had to pull the phone away from her ear when he laughed. "I've missed that booming laugh of yours, Razor."

"I've missed your sense of humor. They say I don't laugh much. Or talk much."

"Who cares what others think. I don't."

"Yeah, you do. It's why you're in Ireland and why you're pissed at John. I thought you liked the girls."

"Yeah, I do. I'm married to one."

"A wife and John?"

"And my daughter's father."

"No wonder you got problems. Most people can't handle one spouse or significant other."

Sam smiled. "I handle them fine. It's just . . . I have medical issues too. It doesn't help."

"Seizures."

"Did you read my book?" Sam asked him.

"Maybe."

"Give me your address, and I'll send you an autographed copy."

"Hmm. I might do that," he told her.

"Thank you, Razor. I needed a distraction. And thank you for what you do to help our fellow vets."

"I've been keeping track of your work, Barrett. Not your personal life but your work. I'm proud to have served with you and proud of what you've done. Sorry about it ending early. I'll bet you could have run the air force better than some. Hell, I'll bet you would have made one helluva chairman of the Joint Chiefs."

Sam was floored by the compliment. "Uh, thanks, Razor. If you need anything—"

"I need you to take care of yourself and check out Be the One on the Legion's website. Legion dot org slash be the one." Then he remembered. "They got a good podcast too. Tango Alpha Lima."

"I get it, Razor."

"Sorry. Just want to pay it back."

"You're doing a great job. Thank you. I owe you a beer," Sam said.

"Two beers."

"OK. Two. Bye."

Razor smiled as the call ended. It was good to talk to an old friend, and he was glad she reached out. Which reminded him, he had some phone calls to make. Another thing Jack had told him about was something called buddy checks. Just calling a vet to make sure they were OK or to ask if they needed anything. He'd called some of his SEAL buddies to check in with them. One of his friends was in bad shape. Razor had stayed on the phone with him all night. On his other phone, he'd called the guy's ex-wife, who promised she'd take him to the hospital. She didn't get along with him, but their kids loved him, and she said she'd help. Razor had developed quite a little network among his buddies. He thought back to a conversation he'd had with Eve. She told him he was a good son for returning to help out his family. He thought she'd approve of this as well. Not that he needed anyone's approval.

CHAPTER 10

Part of Razor's therapy was telling his mother about the stress he was under. She agreed to let him sell the cows and said she would go live with his sister, Lori. It had been a big weight off Razor's shoulders. But Martha asked him to hold on to the property, at least for a while. Razor was still living in his mobile home. He'd been looking for a job, but it was tough going. His retirement pay was just getting him by, and he needed to work. He'd gotten back into shape by joining a gym, and he was still volunteering at the American Legion post.

Two days later, he received a call from a blocked caller. "Who is this?"

"Hammer." Another SEAL buddy. Hammer and Razor went through Basic Underwater Demolition/SEAL (BUD/S) school together. They became friends and helped each other through training. Eventually, they went to different teams and lost touch, but they'd always have that connection.

"Hammer? Long time, buddy," Razor said.

"Yeah. Spoke to a mutual friend a little bit ago. Said I should ring you."

"Who?"

"Barrett," Hammer replied.

Razor smiled. "Barrett. Good troop."

"Got any free time?"

"Yeah. I have a lot of that recently." Razor sighed.

"How'd you like to help me kick Little John's ass, then take a trip across the pond to visit Barrett? Your passport good?" Hammer asked him.

"Yeah. When?" Razor didn't hesitate. A change of scenery would be nice. The therapist he'd been seeing even suggested it in their last session. He'd considered heading down to Galveston, but this would be better. He could reconnect with old friends, and he'd never been to Ireland. Again, Eve entered his mind, but Norfolk was three hours south by car from DC. He talked himself out of going there. It was too late. She'd never forgive him for what he'd texted her that night he got trashed. He was a bit surprised she hadn't tried harder to get in touch with him. She probably had a boyfriend and thought it best to just cut off contact. He growled to himself, *Eve Patterson, you drive me crazy. I'm sorry for being an ass.*

Hammer interrupted his thoughts. "We can spin up whenever you're ready."

"Great. Let me take care of a few things here. I just need a couple of days or so. Send me the details," Razor told him. He was looking forward to getting away.

"You bet." Hammer disconnected the call.

Razor let Jack know he'd be out of town visiting some friends. He didn't want Jack to worry if he didn't contact him for a couple of weeks. Jack was glad to hear he was reconnecting with old friends and reminded him to call his therapist and him if he needed. Then he went to talk to the neighbor whose husband was interested in the land. Razor explained that his mother wasn't ready to sell, but he made a deal that if the man helped him sell the cows, or the bull, he'd get first crack at buying the property. He could also keep any eggs the chickens laid when they were ready. Razor wasn't sure about selling the whole property. He had thought about keeping the part with the house on it. Then Razor called Lori and told her he was going out of town and wasn't sure when he'd be back. Lori told Razor to bring his mother up whenever he was ready. Because Martha was planning to move in with Lori and her family anyway, they loaded his truck with some things she wanted to keep and headed to Athens, Texas. Lori had a room ready for Martha by the time they arrived.

"I really appreciate this, Lori," Razor told her when they arrived at his sister's house.

"I'm sorry about what you went through, Zack," Lori said.

"It was more than just the farm and losing Dad. It was stuff I did and saw on missions that came back to haunt me. All of it just built up, and I didn't deal with it the way I should have. I'm sorry I let Dad down."

"Zack. You did not let Dad down. You came back to help, and you did. I didn't know how much help they really needed. We should have hired someone to help you."

"When I get back, we'll see how Mom feels about the property. Their neighbors will keep an eye on things while I'm gone." He stayed for a few hours and then drove back home. The next morning he locked up the house and checked all the gates, then drove to George Bush Intercontinental Airport in Houston.

It was a three-hour flight direct to Reagan National Airport, where Hammer was waiting for him. It wasn't hard for Hammer to spot him as he came out of the tunnel from the plane. He towered over everyone. "Sasquatch," Hammer said. Then he laughed when he saw the patch on Razor's ball cap. It was a black-and-white American flag with a sasquatch walking in the forest. Perfect for him. Hammer smiled and gave him a hug. "How's it going, buddy? Love the patch," Hammer said. Shorter than Razor at six feet, Hammer was wearing jeans and a T-shirt, which his muscular arms filled out. He also wore a beard, although it wasn't quite as long and thick as Razor's.

"Thanks. It's good."

"Let's get a beer," Hammer said. They went to a restaurant in the airport and caught up. "Heard you went through a rough patch."

"Yeah, but I'm better," Razor told him as he took a sip of his beer. Looking into the glass, he told Hammer what happened. Therapy had made it easier for him to talk about it. Even though he hadn't seen Hammer in years, the military connection made it more comfortable for Razor to talk to him. "I went back home to help my parents with the farm. My dad had these cows for an agriculture exemption on his taxes. The cows were fine, but this damn bull was a pain in the ass. Kept jumping the fence and getting out. The house is old and needed repairs. My parents just couldn't keep up with it all." He paused and then took another sip of the beer. "Then my dad passed, and . . . well, the nightmares didn't help either. Mission shit, you know?" he said, looking at Hammer.

"Yeah. Sometimes I have nightmares about the mission I got hurt on. Being around the guys helps me. Having that connection to other SEAL team members. I don't necessarily have to talk to them, but knowing they're around if I need to makes it easier."

Razor raised his glass. "You're a wise man, Hammer."

"No, just lucky enough to stay close to other team members. If I'd have moved away like you did . . . who knows." Hammer gave Razor a friendly punch in the arm. "You can always call me, buddy."

"Thanks. The same to you."

"Did Barrett tell you what happened?" Hammer asked, changing the subject.

"Yeah. Must have been bad for Little John to take the kids and leave."

"Yeah. How many kids does she have?"

"Uh, five? Three adults, a fifteen-year-old with Little John, and a baby girl with someone else," Razor told him.

"Hey, how did you meet her?" Hammer asked.

Razor smiled and scratched his beard. "My team was at Bagram when some shit went down. I saw what she did to earn her Silver Star. It was fucked up. They sent us to another area of the base. But I saw enough. Assholes should have given her the MOH. We didn't really meet then. She was hurt and got evacuated out. But later we were on a mission together in Sweden. What about you? How did you meet?"

"Little John called me to assist on an off-book mission. Getting a kid and his mom out of Afghanistan. Met her wife on that one."

"No shit. That was you?" Razor asked, surprised by his response.

"What do you mean?"

"It's in the book," Razor told him.

"What book?"

"Her book. Her daughter wrote it."

"You can read?" Hammer laughed as he teased him.

"No. Audiobook, asshole," Razor said without missing a beat.

Hammer continued in a soft voice. "Anyway, that one, and then John called again when her kid was"—he looked around—"captured in Ukraine by Russians. The agency was going to leave him and his spotter there, so we went and got him. She took out two Russians from over seven hundred meters."

"It's in the book. Sort of redacted, and she changed names."

"Then John called again. She used herself as a decoy and was captured by Serbians. The kid, John, and I went to get her. The kid handled it. Not bad for air force. Barrett is something else." He smiled.

"Yeah, she's a helluva woman."

"Pays in cash too. You should do off-book missions with her."

"She paid you?"

"I would have done it for free," Hammer said, draining his glass. "Enough about Barrett. You want to go kick Little John's ass? Or maybe just have a beer?"

"Yeah. Should we call him or just show up?" Razor asked, paying the tab for both of them.

"Whatever. We could show up at the Pentagon and cause trouble." Hammer smiled mischievously.

Razor growled. "No trouble."

"OK. There's a restaurant called Epic Smokehouse near the Pentagon. We can eat and get a beer there."

Razor pulled up their menu and decided that it was acceptable. "Looks good."

"He won't have his cell phone. I'll call him at the office." Hammer dialed the operator and was connected to John's office. Trying to disguise his voice, he said, "General Burke, you need to come to the Epic Smokehouse in one hour so that we can kick your ass for Annie Oakley."

"Who is . . . Hammer?"

"Yeah, Razor is here too. Can you meet us for a beer?"

"Love to. One hour at the Epic Smokehouse," John said.

*****

John walked in, and because he was in his air force uniform, the guys stood at attention and saluted him. John laughed and returned the salute, and they shook hands. "Hammer and Razor. It's really good to see you. You guys ever shave?"

"No," Razor said.

John laughed and sat down. "So Sam called you?"

"Yeah. Needed to hear a friendly voice," Hammer told him.

"Interesting. What did she say?" John asked.

"Private," Razor said.

"Yeah. We're not getting in the middle of it. But we're sorry you guys are having issues."

"What exactly are you general of at the Pentagon?" Razor asked John.

John told them his full title and job description. "So what's with the visit?" Then John became concerned. "Sam didn't call for a mission, did she?"

"What if she did? Do you care?" Razor asked protectively.

John turned slowly and looked at him. "Thought you didn't want to get involved? And for the record, yes, I care. We have a son. She has a baby."

"It's not a mission," Hammer said, trying to ease the tension.

John took a breath. "You guys only know her on the battlefield. Her personal life is complicated. She's been through a lot."

"Read the book," Razor told him.

"Yeah, well, more has happened since then. Why are you guys here?"

"She called us. Just to talk. Misses the baby."

Again, John took a deep breath, not sure how much to share. "She treated us like crap. Her wife and I are used to it. But Andrew—that's the baby's father—isn't used to it. We both said some things, and she told me to take everyone and leave. So I did. It was supposed to be a wake-up call for her. I let it go for too long." John looked at Hammer. "Remember her oldest son, Lex?" Hammer nodded. "He went over to see her. It didn't go well, and she ran away."

"Barrett doesn't run from shit," Razor said.

John was getting angry with Razor's attitude. He leaned over and whispered, "Fuck you."

Razor stood and so did John. They glared at each other from across the table.

"Easy, fellas. Sit down, General," Hammer said.

John needed to be careful. He was in uniform, and he was a high-ranking officer. Getting into a fight in public could cost him his job. He sat, but Razor kept his eyes on him.

"Sit down, Razor," Hammer said.

"Apologize," Razor said to John.

"For what?" John asked.

"Calling her chickenshit."

"I never said that."

"You said she ran away." Razor stood his ground.

Then John realized something. "Oh my god. You're in love with her. Another man falls under the spell of Samantha Barrett."

"No. It's respect. I know what she did. She's a hero."

John didn't want to argue. "Fine, I apologize." When Razor sat down, John told him, "Missions are different from life, Razor. I've worked with both of you on joint missions. I'd take a bullet for either of you. Hell, I've taken a bullet for her. This is personal. This is what she does. She—" Razor growled at him, making sure he didn't say it again. "She leaves. This time she left the country." John was drinking iced tea but ordered a scotch when the server came around.

"We didn't come here to stir up trouble," Hammer said. "Razor needed to get away—"

John cut him off. "Get away or run away?"

"Fuck you," Razor said.

Now it was Hammer who'd had enough. "Shut up, both of you. We've all had our issues. Sam contacted us because she couldn't reach out to you or anyone else."

"She'll come home eventually," John told them. "She calls her psychiatrist."

Razor remembered something from the conversation he'd had with her. "She said she'd been through the same stuff I went through."

"What does that mean?" John asked.

"Suicide."

John stared at him, and his face softened. "I didn't know, Razor. Sorry."

"I'm OK. What about her?"

"It was after she had the baby. I don't even remember what started it. Oh, it was a night terror. She had one and choked Andrew. Then she took off and tried to get a cop to shoot her."

"Jesus," Hammer said.

"Cops brought her home, and she got a gun. Found her with it in one hand and the baby in the other."

"Shit," Razor mumbled.

"She never would have hurt the baby. But she gave me a heart attack. Literally. Had to go to the hospital," John said, subconsciously reaching for his heart. "Let me tell you about your hero. She gets sucked into missions and then puts herself in harm's way." He looked at Hammer. "That mission we went on to rescue her in Serbia? Some bastard raped her. Then she slept with the British agent who was undercover on that mission and dragged her wife along for fun. Then she meets the kid, Andrew, in Hawaii. She gets pregnant and buys the house next door for him and the baby. I had to cut the baby out of her in the middle of the night, and she almost died." John was on a roll and didn't stop. "We went to an embassy party, and she slept with the bartender, the president of Ireland, her wife, and me. That's what the fight was about. Didn't find out until the way home."

"Yeah, but you . . ." Razor wasn't sure what to say.

"I'm used to her screwing around. Andrew wasn't. He took it hard. I tried to explain that to her. I'll admit I called her something I shouldn't have. We fought, and she told me to take everyone and leave. I did."

"You weren't supposed to stay away," Razor told him. "Her words."

"It's easy to Monday morning quarterback," John told him. He finished his scotch. "I have to get back. I'll get this." He stood to leave.

"John, I didn't know all that," Razor said.

"We're OK, Razor. It was nice to get some of that out."

Razor stood, extended his hand, and pulled John in for a hug. "Call me, anytime."

"Thanks. Hammer, good to see you."

"Take care, brother." They shook hands and hugged.

"How long you guys in town for?"

"Fly out tomorrow."

"So she calls, and you go running?" John said.

"No, it's a beer run," Razor said.

"Guinness," Hammer added. "We had vacation time to use."

"I need a change. Even for a week or so. Ireland is better than Galveston. Never been there."

John smirked. "She's in Dublin. Staying with the president of the country. Actually, she's screwing the president," John said.

Razor didn't acknowledge that. Hammer didn't either. "How's the boy?" Razor said, changing the subject.

John smiled. "Jonathan. Great kid. Couldn't be prouder. I have a daughter, too, Emily. Wrapped around my finger."

"A daughter?"

"Yeah, her mother is . . . well, that's a story for another time. Too many spoilers." John smiled. "It was great to see you guys. Stay safe, and let's get together when we all have more time."

"You bet," Hammer said.

"Got a message for Star girl?" Razor asked.

John sighed. "No. Don't worry, it'll work out. She'll come home sooner or later."

"Take care, Little John," Hammer told him. They all shook hands again, and John went back to work. Hammer looked at Razor. "Hmm. What do you think?"

"I think we definitely need to check on Barrett." Razor sighed. "Everyone has different shit they go through. Some more than others. Barrett called two guys she hasn't seen in years. She needs an in-person buddy check."

As they left the restaurant, Hammer said, "Yeah. Uh, what John said. About Barrett."

"What?"

"Are you in love with her?"

Razor kept walking. "When's our flight?" he asked, ignoring Hammer's question.

"Tomorrow afternoon."

"Want to raise some hell?"

"A little. Let's go find some women," Hammer said, grinning.

CHAPTER 11

They didn't exactly raise hell. Finding a sports bar, they ordered a couple of beers.

"I feel bad for them," Razor said.

"Who?"

"Little John and Star girl."

"Sounds like they have a complicated relationship. I mean, she's married with three adult kids and has two kids by two other men. Not to mention the fact that she still has sex with those men."

"You don't know that," Razor said.

"John lives with her and her wife, and the baby's father lives next door. Come on, don't be naïve," Hammer said.

"I'm not saying she's a saint," Razor told him. "It doesn't change the fact that she's a great soldier. I respect that."

"Yeah. But like some of us, we have trouble managing our personal lives."

"If the government wanted you to have a spouse, they would have issued you one."

"Are you sure you don't have feelings for her, fanboy?" Hammer teased him.

Razor gave a low growl. "Pool table is open."

"All right, I get it. Hey, I went into the Rally Point before coming up here. Ran into some of your old teammates," Hammer said as they walked to the pool table.

Razor didn't say anything. He missed the guys.

"They said to tell you hello and to stop by if you get down that way."

After he took a shot, Razor asked, "You miss it?"

"I'm a contractor and help them out. Teaching the newbies and helping with training. It fills a bit of the void. I get to see my boy more," Hammer said, watching Razor sink two balls.

"That's good."

"Heard you had a girl before you left," Hammer said, trying to gather some intelligence.

"Of course you did." The one thing you could count on at a military base or nearby was gossip.

"You miss her?"

Razor sighed and missed a shot. "Your shot."

"Guppy said—"

"Shut up about it. It's over." Razor didn't want to talk about Eve. He had mixed feelings about her. Maybe he should have tried harder to have kept in touch. Maybe she was better off without him. Razor lined up an easy shot but missed. "Damn. I need a drink." He walked to the bar and ordered a shot of whiskey.

"Hey, man, I didn't mean to bring up—"

"Forget it." Razor ordered a shot for Hammer and another for himself.

Tapping their glasses, Hammer said, "To old friends, past and present." They downed the drinks. "Those girls have been eyeing us." Hammer nodded toward some women at a table across the bar from them. "Want to buy them a drink?"

"No."

"Come on, we'll buy them a drink and challenge them to a game of pool."

Razor sighed. He wasn't really in the mood, but the distraction might be good for him. "OK, just pool and a drink."

"Attaboy." Hammer slapped him on the back. They walked over to the women and bought them a round, then asked if they wanted to play pool.

Agreeing, they all went back to the pool table, and Razor racked the balls. One of the women gravitated toward Hammer and began flirting with him. The other wasn't sure about Razor.

"How tall are you?" she asked.

"Six five," he responded. "How tall are you?"

She smiled. "Five five."

Razor was friendly, but he wasn't in the mood for anything more than harmless flirting. When he sat on a stool, the woman stood next to him and placed her hand on his thigh. His manners kicked in, and he stood. "Sorry, have a seat."

"Wow, thanks. You're not from here, are you?"

"Texas. Used to work down near Norfolk." Razor watched as Hammer showed his woman how to line up her shot. He was leaning over her and had one hand on her waist.

"What do you do, Razor?" she asked.

"Retired military."

"Oh."

The way she reacted made it sound like she wasn't a fan. "What about you?"

"I work for the ACLU," she told him.

"You're an attorney?"

"No, just a worker bee. But I'm taking classes and hope to get my law degree someday."

"Good." Things became awkward and uncomfortable.

"Uh, will you excuse me? Ladies' room." She set her drink down, then went over to her friend and whispered in her ear. Her friend smiled at Hammer and gave him a quick kiss. Then they headed to the restroom.

Hammer walked over to Razor and said, "So how's it going?"

"I don't think it's going to work."

"Just relax and have fun. You don't have to marry her."

Razor wanted to leave. He felt like going back to the hotel and just having a few drinks and watching TV. But he didn't want to abandon his friend. He knew Hammer could take care of himself, but buddies didn't ditch each other unless the buddy said it was OK. He sat down as they waited for the women to return.

Razor took a big gulp of his beer and asked Hammer if he wanted another one. Heading to the bar, he ordered another round for all of them.

"Razor, I . . ." The woman came up behind him and stopped talking when he turned around. "Uh, I don't think—"

"It's fine, Dee," Razor told her. The bartender set the drinks down, and Razor handed her one. "No hard feelings."

Dee thought he'd be upset for wasting his time. "You seem like a nice guy. I just—"

"It's OK. I'm flying out tomorrow anyway."

"Let me help carry these," she said, grabbing her friend's drink. "Where are you flying? Back home?"

"No. We're going to check on a friend in Ireland."

"Ireland! Beautiful country. I was there just a few years ago." She seemed more than happy to talk about traveling and Ireland. Telling Razor the things he had to see in different cities, she stuck around. Razor glanced at Hammer, who was kissing the woman he was with.

"Looks like they hit it off," Razor commented.

"Yeah."

"He's a good guy. You don't have to be concerned." Razor wanted to make sure she wouldn't worry about her friend.

Suddenly, Hammer was standing in front of him with his arm around the woman's waist. "You guys want to take this party back to the hotel?"

"You know, I think I'm ready to call it a night," Dee said.

"Dee?" her friend said. She pulled her aside, and they talked.

Razor looked at Hammer. "It's cool. She told me some places to check out in Ireland."

"You sure?"

"Yeah. I'll sit in the bar or something. Call or text when it's safe to come up." They were sharing a room with two beds.

Dee and her friend came back. Razor looked at Dee and said, "Can I get you a cab or something?"

"That'd be great. Thanks."

"No problem." Outside, Razor flagged down a taxi, then opened the door for her. "It was nice meeting you, Dee."

"You too, Razor." She hesitated, looking back for her friend.

"I'll make sure she gets home."

Dee smiled. "I believe you." She grabbed his shirt, pulled him down, and kissed him. "Have fun in Ireland."

"Thanks." Razor started to close the door but heard someone call his name.

"Wait up!" Hammer yelled as he approached with the woman. They kissed for what seemed like forever. Finally, she got in the cab next to Dee. Razor turned and looked at Hammer.

"What?" Hammer said.

Razor just shook his head.

"Ready to call it?" Hammer asked.

"Yeah."

*****

They flew out the next afternoon and landed in Dublin the following morning with the time change.

"Hey, I got a plan for Barrett. This is what we'll do. I'll call her and tell her to go to this place called the Brazen Head, then hang up. She won't know we're in town. We'll sneak up and surprise her."

"Weak, but OK," Razor said.

"You make a plan."

"Not a planner. Door-kicker," Razor told him.

"Then don't complain," Hammer said.

*****

Sam's phone rang, and she tried to focus on what the caller ID said but couldn't. "I need to give more people their own ringtones." She ignored it. Then it rang again. "Keeva!"

"Yes, ma'am?" Keeva said, coming into the room.

"Who is calling me? I can't read it."

"It says Hammer."

"Hammer? Really? Yeah, you wouldn't know that," Sam said, realizing there was no way Keeva could pull that name out of thin air. It rang again, and Sam showed Keeva her phone.

"Hammer," Keeva said again.

"Hello, Hammer," Sam said after taking a while to answer the call. She was sitting at a desk at Farmleigh, where dignitaries and guests of the nation of Ireland stayed. But the president of Ireland, Roisin Doyle, arranged for Sam to stay there when she wasn't sleeping with her at Áras an Uachtaráin, the residence of the president of Ireland.

"Are you busy?" Hammer asked, thinking she might be.

"No."

"I need you to go somewhere for me," Hammer said, getting to the point of his call.

"What? I'm in Dublin."

"One hour, the Brazen Head. Be there." He hung up.

"What? Hammer? Hammer!" Sam was confused. She set the phone down and sighed. "I'm too old for missions.

Keeva!" She called for her assistant. Roisin had hired someone to help Sam with anything she needed. She didn't like it at first, but Keeva was especially helpful now that Sam had had surgery on one of her eyes.

"Ma'am, there's an intercom right there." Keeva pointed to the landline and one of the buttons.

"Oh. Why didn't you say so? Yelling takes me back to my military days."

"I see. Tin cans and a string? Or Morse code?" Keeva teased.

Sam glared at her, and Keeva squirmed in her seat. Then Sam broke into a smile. "Good one. You're funny. I need to go to the Brazen Head in forty-five minutes."

"Yes, ma'am."

*****

Forty-five minutes later, the driver Roisin had given Sam pulled up to the Brazen Head. Sam told Keeva and the driver to stay in the car. They all waited. Sam wasn't sure, but years as a federal investigator and sometimes CIA officer made her cautious. It was probably safe, but she wasn't going to take any chances. She kept watching for anything or anyone out of place.

"You know, this is Ireland's oldest pub," Keeva said to Sam.

"Cool," Sam said, watching the entrance. She looked at her watch, but with the eye patch and poor vision in her good eye, she couldn't focus and asked Keeva what time it was. Satisfied, Sam said, "OK, we can go in."

They got out of the vehicle, and Sam told Keeva to stay behind her as she entered the pub first. It was busy and music was playing. Sam looked around but didn't see anyone she knew. The hair on the back of her neck stood up, and she felt a hand on her shoulder. She grabbed the fingers, twisted them, and took the man to his knees.

"Annie Oakley!" Hammer said.

"Hammer! What the hell!" Sam released him, and then someone bear-hugged her from behind and lifted her. He set her down, and she turned to see Razor. "Razor."

"Star girl." They all hugged.

Keeva didn't know what to think about the two large burly men surprising Sam. They looked as if they had just returned from the woods.

"Keeva, these are two friends of mine. Hammer and Razor. Boys, this is Keeva Murray. My assistant."

"Nice to meet you, ma'am," Hammer said and smiled.

Razor towered over her and said, "Hi."

"Uh, hello." She shook Hammer's hand and held hers out to Razor, who just stared at her. Sam elbowed him in the stomach, and he shook her hand.

"Come on. We have some seats at the bar," Hammer said. "We didn't know you'd bring company."

Razor said to Keeva, "Sit here, please." Hammer and Sam looked at him as he gave Keeva his stool and stood at the bar.

"Thank you," Keeva replied in her Irish accent.

"What are you guys doing here?" Sam asked.

"Beer run," Razor said, and Keeva laughed. "Drink?" he asked her.

Sam leaned over to Hammer and asked, "What is happening?"

"I'm not sure, but I think he's smitten," he whispered back. "What'll it be?"

"What are those draughts?" Sam asked him to read the beers for her, then ordered a Brazen Red.

"What happened to your eye?" Hammer said, pointing to her patch.

"Detached retina. I had surgery and will be fine. I can't believe you guys came all this way."

"Yeah, well, next time you run away, would you go to Tahiti?" Hammer said.

Sam laughed. "I'll try." She placed a hand on his. "It's good to see you both. So what are you really doing here? I'm not available for any missions."

"You called us. We just wanted to make sure you were OK. Besides, we had some vacation to use."

"Bullshit. You don't fly across the ocean to check on someone."

Hammer took a sip of his beer. "Sasquatch needed a break. He went through a rough time."

"Yeah, he told me," Sam said.

"When you told me to call him, I found out where he was and made a call to a friend of a friend. They gave me the scoop on him. It was bad. He's better but sometimes getting away from things helps." He looked in her one eye. "Is it helping you?"

"Screw you, Hammer. Did you talk to John?"

"As a matter of fact, we did stop and have lunch with a certain general." Hammer watched as a man came up to Keeva and asked if he could buy her a drink. Razor had been leaning on the bar, but he stood straight up and glared at the man. He left.

"Darts," Razor said to Sam.

"I can't see shit with one eye. Why don't you and Keeva play?" Sam said. She could have played but wanted to see if Razor and Keeva would hit it off. Razor looked at her, knowing what she was doing, but he asked Keeva to play anyway. He actually said an entire sentence when he asked her. Sam smiled as they walked off.

"Huh, it only took flying across the ocean and an Irish girl to get him back in the saddle," Hammer said.

"What do you mean?" Sam asked.

"I heard he'd fallen for a girl but left her behind when he moved back to Texas. They said she was good for him."

Sam was silent and sipped her beer.

*****

"Um, I have darts," Keeva said, pulling some from her purse as they waited for an open board. It was only a few minutes. "Five oh one, three oh one, or something else?"

"Uh, teach me three oh one?"

Keeva smiled at him. "It's easy. First one out wins. We start at three hundred and one and subtract the points."

"Math." He made a face, and Keeva laughed again. "Ladies first."

"Thanks. Oh, just to make sure you know the board. Fifty, twenty-five, this area is double, and this is treble. Triple." She pointed to the sections as she explained them.

"Got it."

Keeva put the flights on her darts and threw one. *Twenty-five, treble twenty is sixty, and twenty. Subtracting that from 301 makes 196.*

Razor growled.

Keeva brought the darts back and handed them to him. He felt the weight of the dart and lined up his shot. Twenty, treble twenty, and five.

"Two hundred sixteen," Razor said.

"Yeah," she said, taking the darts from him when he retrieved them. Keeva had a feeling he was toying with her. Playing the big dumb ape. She got her score down to nineteen, and Razor had twenty-seven points. It was Razor's turn, and he hit the twenty. Then he looked at her and threw the dart, hitting the nineteen, which was next to the seven.

"Over," Razor said. Keeva hit the twenty and won. "You win."

"What do I get for winning?"

"What do you want?" Razor asked.

"A kiss," she said. He leaned down and gave her a kiss. "I think you let me win," Keeva told him as she stared up into his brown eyes.

He growled and cracked a smile. They made their way through the crowd to Sam and Hammer for another drink. Sam said something to make Razor laugh. He talked a little more, and his sentences became longer than one or two words once he was comfortable.

"How do you know each other?" Keeva asked Sam.

"His team helped me on a mission in Sweden. I call it Operation Princess."

"Princess? And now a president," Keeva teased.

"No, that was a mission. Totally different," Sam snapped back as she clarified.

"Sorry, ma'am. I didn't mean to offend," Keeva apologized.

Sam sighed. "You didn't. I'm sorry."

"Hey, are you OK?" Hammer asked.

"No. I have a TBI, seizures, and PTSD. I'm far from OK," Sam told him.

"We didn't come here to stir up trouble. We can go," Hammer said.

"No. I'm sorry. What did asshat say?"

Razor laughed.

Hammer smiled. "If you mean John, he just told us what happened. We're not judging."

"Do you think I care?" Sam asked him.

"No."

"Little John misses you. He made a mistake and stayed away too long," Razor said.

"I'll go back when I'm ready. I'm not ready," Sam told them.

It was getting late. Sam's phone rang, but she ignored it.

Keeva answered it instead. "Ma'am? It's for you."

Sam took the phone. "Sorry. Some friends showed up in town. We're at the Brazen Head. Come on down and meet them."

Razor took Keeva's hand and led her away from the others. They stood against a wall on the other side of the pub.

"Where are you from, Razor?"

"Texas," Razor said.

"Tell me about the mission," she said, taking a sip of her drink.

"I was a navy frogman." Razor stared into her eyes.

"Frogman?" Keeva asked.

"United States Navy SEAL."

"Oh. Impressive."

"Not really."

"Yes, it is. Special Forces, right? I heard the attrition rate is very high."

He shrugged. "Do you work for the president?"

"Sort of, but I'm the colonel's assistant. I'm hoping to work for the president later."

"Hmm. You have pretty hair," Razor told her, reaching up and touching a few strands.

"Thank you. I like your beard and that patch on your hat." Keeva glanced over at Sam. She saw Roisin hiding under a ball cap with her hair in a ponytail. "Oh, come on. That's my boss over there. I want you to meet her."

"I already know Colonel Barrett."

"The president," she whispered.

"Meet the president?"

"Yeah, it's fine."

Razor followed Keeva back over to Sam, and Keeva said to the president, "Uh, ma'am. I didn't think you were coming."

"She changed her mind," Sam said, handing Keeva's phone back to her. Sam wanted to discreetly send Keeva a text. She started to but couldn't see the keyboard because, like her watch, it was blurry. She sighed. "I really need glasses. Come with me, Keeva. Ladies' room." As they walked away, Sam stopped and said, "You can have the rest of the night off."

Keeva was surprised. "Ma'am?" She didn't know why she'd dismissed her.

"Go have fun with Razor. He's a good guy."

Keeva stammered. "I . . . why . . . uh . . ."

"Oh my God, just go have fun. Get laid." Sam walked into the ladies' room.

Keeva returned to Razor. "Did they introduce you?"

"Yes."

"You met the president of Ireland," she whispered.

"Yeah, she seems nice."

"Come on." She took his hand and started to lead him outside the pub.

Razor stopped her. "Wait. I need to take of something first. My main reason for coming here." He walked back inside and over to Sam, who had just returned to the bar. "May I speak to you privately?"

"Sure." Sam walked outside. "It's crowded, and I can hear you better out here."

"This is fine."

"Something wrong?" she asked, looking up at him.

He wasn't sure how to start. "I . . . uh . . ."

"Spit it out, Razor. What's the problem?"

"I don't want to make you angry."

Sam sighed. "Are you going to lecture me?"

"No."

"Say what you have to say," Sam told him.

"You were a great soldier. I saw you in action. In Afghanistan and that mission in Sweden. That's our outlet. But you got hurt and I retired, so we don't have that anymore."

"Thought this wasn't a lecture. What's your point?"

"Forget it. Your personal life is your business."

Sam could tell he was being sincere. "Razor, I know my life is a mess. I've made choices that have me here in Ireland, away from my family. This is temporary. I don't know when, but I'll go back."

"John loves you."

Sam looked away so that he wouldn't see the anger and hurt in her one eye. "I know." She wiped her cheek.

"I didn't mean to upset you. You're a smart woman. You don't need to take advice from a stupid lug like me."

Sam turned back and punched him in the chest. "Hey, you aren't a stupid lug. I appreciate your concern."

"Are you OK, Sam? Don't lie to me."

"I'm better than when I called you. I have good days and bad days. Razor, I have a TBI. I have mood swings and get angry. I'm short-tempered, and I take it out on those around me. I use sex as an outlet, a release, or a distraction."

Razor's face turned a little red when she spoke of sex.

Sam chuckled. "Did I embarrass you?"

"I just didn't expect that."

"I have flaws, but I love my family, Razor. I'm still angry with John for taking them away."

"You told him to."

"I didn't think they'd stay away. There's something else I'm not sure you're aware of."

"What?"

"That night he had my daughter and was coming down the stairs. I went to stop him from taking her, and he pushed me."

"He pushed you down the stairs?" That made Razor angry.

"Settle down. I've done worse to him. I get violent sometimes. It was just a couple of steps to get me out of his way."

"Doesn't matter."

"I don't care about the push. It's what happened after. I fell, and when I went to stand, I rolled my ankle. Not the first time. I didn't take care of myself or get help. I don't know how, but I developed sepsis and was barely able to call 911." She paused as she thought about it. "No one came to the hospital. No one." Sam wiped the tear from her cheek.

He saw a vulnerable side of Sam. A side he hadn't seen in Afghanistan or Sweden. Yes, he'd read her book and there were plenty of emotional parts in there. But to see her wipe the tear from her cheek made him respect her even more. "I'm sorry. I didn't know. That was cruel. No matter what, I don't think you deserved that." Suddenly, he pulled her close and hugged her. Then he released her just as quickly. "Sorry."

"Don't apologize for hugging a friend. Thank you." Sam reached out and embraced him again. This time holding him longer. "You're a good man, Razor. A very good friend."

"Zack."

Sam let him go and looked up at him. "Zack."

"Don't share that. It's classified."

"You don't want me to tell anyone your real name?"

"No. I have a reputation," Razor said gruffly.

"So do I. At Quantico and the Pentagon they called me Barrett the Beast. I threw phones and cups at walls."

"You have anger issues."

"Which is one reason why I have a psychiatrist. I can't promise I won't go down the rabbit hole again. But I don't want you to worry about me. I'll get through this."

"Keep talking to your doctor. Call me if you need to. Day or night, anytime. Or call Hammer. Promise me," Razor said.

"I promise. Thank you for coming. It means a lot." She smiled at him. "Now go take my assistant home or back to your hotel. She needs a good lay."

"Come on, Barrett. You're a lady and an officer." He turned red again.

Sam laughed. "I'm just one of the guys, Zack." As they walked inside, she said, "Be safe, Razor." She made her way back to the bar where Hammer and Roisin were.

Keeva found Razor, and they left the bar. She pulled him down for a kiss. "How tall are you?"

"Why does everyone ask that? Six foot five."

"Wow. So where would you like to go?"

He smiled. "Your place."

"Can't. I have a room in the president's residence."

"So?"

She looked at him and smiled. "Oh, what the hell." She flagged down a cab. "Áras an Uachtaráin," she told the driver.

"Ma'am, it's closed," he said in Gaelic.

"I work and live there. It's OK," she told him in the same language.

"Yes, ma'am."

Razor leaned over and kissed her. "Talk more Gaelic."

"What do you want me to say?" she asked in Gaelic.

Razor smiled, and they kissed. They made out in the back seat all the way to the residence. They pulled up to the gate and security stopped them.

"Ma'am. Excuse me, ma'am," the cabbie said.

Keeva pulled away from Razor. "Oh, sorry." She rolled down the back window and looked at the guard. "Mick, it's me coming home."

"Oh, Miss Keeva. Uh, does your companion have ID?" Mick asked.

"Razor, do you have ID?"

"Yeah." He reached in his cargo pants pocket and gave her his passport.

"Zachary Wyatt Reston." She smiled and gave it to Mick.

"Razor." They kept staring at each other.

"Sir, if you're going into the residence, I need to check you. Will you step out for a moment, sir?"

"What?" Razor was lost in Keeva's eyes. "Oh, yeah. No problem."

"He needs to run the wand over you. You don't have any weapons, do you?"

"Only my sharp wit," he said, getting out and walking over to Mick. Mick ran the wand over one side and the other, then his front and back. It squealed on his front. He lifted his shirt and showed Mick his big Texas-size belt buckle. He took it off, and Mick checked again. This time the wand squealed near his boots. He took his cowboy boots off, and Mick looked inside and ran the wand over him once more.

"Thank you, sir."

"No problem." Razor waited for his passport while putting his boots and his belt back on.

"You're good to go, sir." Mick handed him his passport.

"Thanks. Let's walk," Razor said to Keeva through the window.

"OK," Keeva said, stepping out of the car.

"How much?" Razor asked the cabbie. Razor paid him and took Keeva's hand. "Tell me about this place."

"I'm not really a tour guide."

"You have to know something about it."

Keeva smiled and started relaying facts about the residence as they walked. She took him around to the private entrance, and they went inside. "Want some wine or something?"

"Or something." He smiled. "Beer?"

"OK." They went into the kitchen, and she looked in the fridge. She grabbed four beers and some cheese and crackers. She gave him the drinks to carry and said, "Follow me." She walked to her room and set the cheese and crackers down. "Oh, for the love of—"

"What?"

"I forgot the bottle opener."

"I got it." He set two beers on a table and then pulled out his keys and opened the other two bottles with the attached opener.

He handed her one and looked around. He didn't see a bed. It was like a living room. A small one but a living room nonetheless.

"Have a seat. Relax," Keeva said.

"I thought you said you have a room."

Keeva laughed. "This is mine."

"Oh." He lifted a cushion off the couch.

"What are you doing?"

"Uh, nothing."

Keeva laughed again, knowing full well he was looking for the bed. "Patience."

Razor put the cushion down and sat next to her. "Sorry."

"Here, try this." She spread some cheese on a cracker and gave it to him.

"Hmm. Good. Whipped cream would have been better." Saying that reminded him of Eve. His face changed, and Keeva noticed. There was a slight sadness in his eyes, but she ignored it.

"Razor. You're a funny guy." Keeva leaned over and gave him a kiss. She moved closer, and he placed his hand on her leg. He put his other hand behind her neck and then gently ran it through her hair. Keeva moved her hand up his leg and under his shirt. His skin was taut and firm. He moved his hand to her shirt. She had removed her suit jacket earlier, so he started on the buttons. For a man with large hands, his dexterity impressed her, along with his body. He began kissing her neck as he moved his hands down each button. He untucked her shirt and finished the last button, kissing her in the middle of her neck. They both knew what this was, and they both needed it. It might be a one-night stand, but for Razor it was more than that. He liked this girl. It was the first time since Eve that he felt anything for another woman. It wasn't the same, but at least he knew he could feel again.

Suddenly, Razor pulled away and took her hand. "Wait."

"What's wrong?" Keeva asked.

"I . . . uh. Are you sure this is what you want? I'm not going to be around."

Keeva smiled. "I'm a big girl. I like you. I don't do this all the time. You could say I'm just following orders." She grinned mysteriously.

"What do you mean?"

"The colonel told me you were a nice guy and that I should get laid."

Razor's eyes narrowed and his forehead wrinkled. Then he smiled. "Well, who am I to disobey orders?" He ran his hand up her arm and brushed his lips over hers.

Razor was wearing a T-shirt under a casual button-down shirt. Keeva didn't even bother with the buttons. Instead, she pulled both shirts up over his head. In Gaelic, she said, "Sweet mother of Mary. You are so hot."

"Uh, I don't know what you said."

"It was a compliment," she said in English.

Razor smiled at her and returned the compliment. "You are a beautiful woman," he said in a different language.

She stopped and looked at him. "What was that?"

"Farsi."

"You are full of surprises." Keeva stood and took his hand. She led him to a door and opened it.

"So are you," he said, looking at the large bedroom. He picked her up and took her to bed.

*****

"Razor, wake up. Razor, wake up!" Keeva pushed his hard body, but he barely moved.

"Hmm."

"I have to work."

He looked at his watch. "It's four in the morning! It's too early."

"I know, but the colonel has to be at the studio for her interview. You need to go."

He growled and sat up. Then he got out of bed. "Wow, you are a specimen," Keeva said, admiring his muscled body.

Ignoring her comment, he said, "Can I get a shower?"

She didn't answer, lost in her own thoughts.

"Keeva."

"Let's shower together." She grabbed his hand and pulled him to the bathroom.

*****

"Come on," Keeva whispered as she led him outside to a waiting car. She'd asked one of the security men to drive him to his hotel. "Thank you. I had a wonderful time last night. The darts, the drinks, and . . ." She smiled.

"Me too. Take care." He kissed her goodbye.

Kimberly A. Biggerstaff © 2025

"If you're ever in Ireland again, look me up." To the driver, she said, "Take him to—"

"Hampton, City Center," Razor told the man.

"Yeah," Keeva said, staring at him.

"Yes, ma'am," the driver said.

Razor smiled at her as they drove off. Keeva waved and ran back inside. Razor had enjoyed being with her. He realized he must have been tired because he didn't wake up early and he didn't dream or have a nightmare. Keeva was nice, and if someone else hadn't crept into his thoughts, he might have considered taking her up on her offer to look her up again. He needed to take a trip to Norfolk.

CHAPTER 12

Razor woke when his phone buzzed and there was a knock on the door. He looked at his watch. Eight o'clock. He shuffled to the door and looked through the peephole. Opening it, he was met with a grin.

"Am I interrupting anything?"

"No," Razor said, letting Hammer inside.

"Have fun last night?"

"Yeah."

"Where did you go?"

"Her place."

"Good for you." Hammer slapped his bare arm. "What time did you get in?"

"Just before five. Barrett had an interview."

"Yeah, morning television. I saw it. Very entertaining. Anyway, do you want to do some exploring today? We came all this way," Hammer said, sitting in a chair.

"Yeah," Razor replied. He made his way toward the bathroom but stopped and looked at Hammer. "Is she OK?"

"Barrett? Yeah. I spoke with the president's man. Conor, I think was his name. Anyway, I told him we were concerned about her."

"And?" Razor waited.

"She's fine. He'll keep an eye on her," Hammer said.

Razor went to the bathroom. Hammer sighed. He knew Razor had a harmless crush on Sam, but he couldn't tell him how he really felt. Sam's personal life was a mess. Mostly due to her own actions. Hammer told Conor, the president's personal aide and best friend, that they were worried about her. Conor promised to intervene if Sam's mental health declined.

*****

A week and a half later, Razor spent the entire flight back to Washington, DC, thinking about what he wanted to do when they returned. Before they landed, Razor turned to Hammer and said, "You live in Norfolk, right?"

"Yeah. I told you I contract with the navy. Help the teams with their training."

"Sounds fun," Razor said.

"Keeps me busy and supplements my retirement. No deployments."

"Hmm."

Razor wanted to go to Norfolk or Virginia Beach and hoped Hammer would get the hint.

"Why don't you come stay with me for a few days? We'll visit the old haunts. Maybe stop in at the Rally Point."

"You sure?" Razor asked.

"Yeah. It's no problem."

"Thanks."

*****

Hammer had driven the less-than-four-hour drive from his home in Norfolk to Reagan National. They found his SUV in the long-term parking lot and drove back to Norfolk. Hammer had a small three-bedroom house. It was an older home, but the interior was modern.

"Nice house," Razor told him as they went inside.

"Thanks. My son, Nicky, has one bedroom when he's here, but you can have the other. This way." Hammer led him down a hall. He opened the door and showed him his son's room. "My boy is twelve. He's into gaming and computers." The room was neat, and there was a computer on the desk with controllers and a headset. "I try to get him outside when he visits. He likes to swim."

"Try diving? Not off a board."

"I know what you mean. I've been thinking about that. Maybe getting him PADI certified so we can do that together. Anyway, your room is this one." He took him to another door and opened it. It looked like a home office, with a desk, shelves with an assortment of books, and a small sofa. "That sofa folds out to a bed. Use the closet. Whatever you need. The bathroom is over there. I'll get you some sheets and pillows." He went to the bathroom closet and found some linens for the sofa bed. Then he pulled down a blanket and two pillows. "I don't really have too many guests."

"It's fine. Better than a foxhole. I appreciate it."

"No problem. You can use my truck if you need it."

"I can rent something."

"Wait a bit and see if you really need to. Or . . ." Hammer trailed off, as if remembering something.

"What?"

"Follow me." Hammer led him out to the detached garage. He unlocked the side door, and they went inside. Flipping the light switch on, Razor looked around and smiled. There was a workbench, some weights and a bench, and a motorcycle. "It's old and needs a little work, but if you can get it started, you can use it."

"Nice." Razor walked over to the motorcycle to take a better look.

"You still have a license?"

"Yeah. I just haven't ridden in years. Royal Enfield Interceptor." Razor knelt down, looking at the engine. "Where did you find it?"

"A guy on base got married, and his wife was worried about him riding. They're expecting a kid. I haven't had time to mess with it. Thought of working on it with the boy."

Razor stood up. "Do that." He didn't want to take any kind of father-son time away from Hammer and Nicky.

"No, it's OK. Maybe you can help me get him interested. He's coming over this weekend. You hungry?"

"Yeah."

"We need to go shopping too. Groceries. How about spaghetti?" Hammer asked.

"Yeah, fine. Got a laptop or computer I can use?" Razor asked.

"Sure. Use the one in Nicky's room. The password is Dadisthecoolest! One word, capital *D* and an exclamation point at the end."

Razor growled and rolled his eyes as they went back into the house. "Let me know if you need help," Razor said.

"It's spaghetti. I got it. Let me know if the kid is watching porn," Hammer said.

Razor went to Nicky's room and booted up the computer.

From the kitchen, Hammer yelled, "Don't you start watching porn!"

Razor growled and snickered. "Dad is cool, my ass." Razor checked his email, but there wasn't much. He dumped it all into the trash except for one message from Jack, which he responded to. He let him know he was back in Virginia staying with a friend and that he was doing good. Razor did feel better. Hanging out with Hammer had been therapeutic for him. Hammer understood better than anyone about the missions and the nightmares that sometimes came with them. One night, he'd even told Hammer how bad it had gotten for him. He'd also told him how Jack had gotten him help.

Razor stared at the screen for a minute, then read a few of the news items that came up on the browser. He was stalling. He still had her number in his favorites list on his phone and could call or text. No, he didn't want to do that. It had been too long. Maybe not that long in the grand scheme of things, but a lot had happened, and his last text to her wasn't exactly friendly. Finally, he googled her name. There were a few Eve Pattersons. He scrolled down and found her: Eve Patterson, Patriots & Veterans Realty. He pulled up the website. It was her company. She'd had it for ten years. Built it after establishing herself as a top Realtor in the area. He'd never asked her about work other than a passing question about her day. He wished he had. He had never been to her office either. He began to question their relationship. The effort he'd put into it—or lack thereof. Had it been enough? She'd never told him she'd wanted anything more than what they had. They'd had fun together. They'd gone to the movies, the beach, the Rally

Point, even golfing. They'd fallen asleep on her balcony under the stars. But then his pride would surface, and he'd say or do something stupid. He knew it was his fault, and it usually came before a deployment. But somehow he would always go back to her, tail between his legs, flowers in hand, and an apology on his lips. The first couple of times, she didn't forgive him right away. She made him work for it. But in the end, she always forgave him.

"Spaghetti's ready." Hammer walked in, and Razor closed the browser. "Thinking about moving?" Clearly, he'd seen Eve's Realtor website.

"No."

Hammer let it go. They went to the kitchen and dished up their spaghetti and sauce.

"Parmesan cheese?" Razor asked.

"Fridge. Grab a couple of beers too."

Razor did, and they sat at the kitchen table and ate. After a few minutes, Razor said, "She's a friend."

"What? Who?"

"The Realtor. Old friend." He paused and added, "Old girlfriend."

"Oh. The one the guys told me about. You going to look her up?"

"Maybe. I don't know." Razor wanted to change the subject. "No porn."

"What?"

"The browser history didn't have porn. But he could have cleared it."

"You actually checked?"

Razor shrugged, and Hammer smiled.

*****

Razor wanted Hammer and his boy to be able to get the bike running, so he went out to the garage to figure out what they might need. After checking it over, he made a list. The next day, he told Hammer they had to go to the auto parts store.

"The bike isn't that bad. Minor stuff and a good cleaning."

"Good. Nicky is coming tomorrow, so save something for him. I just want to teach some basic stuff."

"Yeah."

*****

The next day, Nicky ran into the house and bumped into Razor. He looked up at the large man and stepped back. He grabbed a knife from the counter where Razor had been making a sandwich. "Where's my dad, you big hulk! Mom! Call the cops!"

"I'm a friend," Razor said, looking down at the boy.

"Nicky, what's—who are you?" A woman appeared and looked at him.

"Razor. Old SEAL friend," Razor said.

"Nicky. Hey, buddy. Put the knife down. Razor and I went through BUD/S together. He's cool," Hammer said, entering the kitchen. "Hi, Monica."

"Hello, Nick."

"You're huge," Nicky said to Razor.

"I ate my vegetables," Razor said with a straight face as the boy stared at him.

"Razor, this is my ex-wife, Monica, and my son, Nicholas Jr. Nicky."

"Nice to meet you," Razor said to Monica.

"Do you work out?" Nicky asked Razor.

"Yes."

"What do you bench?"

"Two seventy-five."

"Wow. Hey, Dad, Mom says I can get some weights if you show me how to use them without hurting myself."

Hammer looked at his ex-wife and then back at his son. He was surprised. Nicky had never shown interest in weightlifting before. "Yeah, you bet. Go put your stuff away, Nicky." The boy walked off to his room with his backpack.

Razor went back to making his sandwich.

Monica walked to the living room and signaled to Hammer that he should follow. "I didn't know you had company. Is he staying here?"

"Yeah. On my sofa bed in the spare room. Is that a problem?"

"No. I trust you."

"It's not like the old days. We're older and a little more mature."

She smiled. "More mature?"

"A little."

"Did he go with you to Ireland?"

"Yeah. We met up with another old friend. I got to meet the president of Ireland," he bragged.

"Really? Something related to your SEAL days?"

"No. Well, sort of. I mean, the woman we met up with, Sam Barrett, is—"

"Wait a minute." Monica stopped him. "You know Samantha Barrett?"

"Yeah. I went on two missions with her. Off-book. Anyway, Razor knows her, too, and she called us. Having a rough time at home and ran off to Ireland. We went to check on her."

"All the way to Ireland?" Monica asked suspiciously.

"Yeah. We did some sightseeing too. The Guinness brewery, the Jameson distillery, and other stuff. I got Nicky a shirt from Dublin Castle." He forgot the point of the story.

"And you met the president."

"Oh, right. Barrett is"—he made sure Nicky wasn't nearby—"screwing around with her. We met in a pub, and the president came later. Nice lady. How do you know Barrett?" Hammer asked his ex-wife.

"I don't know her personally. I read her book. It was a bestseller, and it seemed interesting. That part about the rogue ATF agent who came after her was gripping."

"Yeah, well . . . what's in the book? Am I in there? Razor said she wrote about the mission I was on to Afghanistan to get a boy and his mother out." It was about fifteen years ago. Hammer had been medically retired from the navy after a mission, but when John had called to ask for his help, Hammer hadn't hesitated. Monica hadn't been happy about it, and it had led to more problems and a divorce shortly before Nicky was born.

"That was you? You idiot. You got shot, didn't you?" She pulled his shirt up and looked at the scar.

"Hey." He tried to push her hands away. "Did she change my name or something?"

"Yes. Called you knucklehead." She grinned at him.

"Very funny. Back to Razor. He's a good guy. Looks scary but a good guy. A Texas gentleman."

"Does he have kids?"

"No."

"He was a SEAL?"

"Yes. Used to be at Virginia Beach. Little Creek. Different team. He's retired and lives in Texas. Anything else you want to know?"

"If Nicky is staying here, I just want to know who else is around. That's not unreasonable."

"I can go to a hotel," Razor said, entering the living room. "Sorry, not eavesdropping."

"No, that's not necessary," Hammer told him. "Is it, Monica? Look, Nicky seems to like him."

"No, it's fine. I hope I didn't offend you . . . Razor."

"No. I get it. Protect the boy." He walked back to the kitchen.

Monica crossed her arms and looked at Hammer. "Is that how he always talks? One- to three-word sentences?"

"No. Well, most of the time. You just have to get to know him."

"OK. Back to Nicky. Show him how to properly lift and maybe you can get him a set of weights for Christmas."

"When did he get interested in weights?"

"I don't know. He's a boy; you ask him. But something may have happened at school. If you find out, let me know."

"Is he getting bullied?" Hammer asked. He'd have no problem making a trip to the school to talk to the principal.

"I don't know. He won't tell me."

"All right. I'll let you know if I learn anything."

"Nicky! I'm leaving," Monica called to him.

"OK, Mom!"

Hammer and Monica found Nicky at the kitchen table watching Razor eat his sandwich. "What's good to eat when you work out?"

"Protein," Razor said.

"Were you on my computer?"

"Yes."

"Were you looking at naughty stuff?"

"No!" Razor said loudly.

Hammer started to interrupt, but Monica stopped him. "I want to hear this," she whispered.

"Do you have kids?"

"No, not married."

"You don't have to be married to have kids."

"Marriage first, then kids," Razor said between bites of his sandwich.

"You were a SEAL, like Dad?"

"Yes."

"You ever kill anyone?"

"I protected my teammates."

"You didn't answer the question."

"Ask your dad," Razor said, taking the last bite of his sandwich and drinking his glass of water.

"I did."

"And?"

"He said sometimes in war you have to do bad stuff. But protecting your team, yourself, and the country is important. It's why we can do what we want here in America. It's not like that in other countries."

"Your dad is right. Women can't go to school in some countries."

"They can't?" Nicky was surprised.

"No. Can't drive either."

Monica had heard enough. Razor seemed like a decent man. "Nicky, I'm going. Do you have everything?"

"Yeah, Mom. I'm squared away."

Hammer smiled, and Razor grunted. Monica came into the kitchen, and Razor stood up, which surprised her.

"Why did you stand up?" Nicky asked.

"Always stand when a lady comes over."

"You could learn a thing or two from him," she told Hammer.

Nicky stood, and Monica kissed him on the cheek. "Be good."

"Mom." He wiped his now red cheek, embarrassed that his mother kissed him in front of Razor.

"It was nice to meet you, Razor."

"You too, ma'am."

Hammer walked Monica to her SUV. "I'll see you on Sunday," Hammer said, holding the door. She started the vehicle. "Monica?"

"Yes?"

He hesitated. "Uh, never mind. See you Sunday." She put the vehicle in reverse and backed down the driveway.

Hammer jumped when Razor whispered in his ear, "Nice lady."

"Shit, Razor. Are you trying to give me a heart attack?"

"Kid asks a lot of questions."

"Yeah, it's how they learn."

"He wants to see me bench," Razor said walking back towards the house.

"Well, let's show him."

CHAPTER 13

On Sunday afternoon, Hammer and Nicky were making some final checks on the bike in the garage.

"Here comes your mom. Go wash up and get your stuff," Hammer told him.

"Aw, man." Nicky stood and looked at the vehicle coming up the driveway. He sighed and went into the house after kicking the ground.

Nicky hung his head all the way to the bathroom. He washed his hands and went to his room. Razor was on the computer.

"You need the computer?"

"No. Mom is here. Time for me to go," he said, picking up some of his things and placing them in his backpack. Sitting on the bed, he let out a deep sigh.

Razor turned in the chair and looked at him. "Something wrong?"

"I had a lot more fun this weekend. I don't want to go. I mean, I never like leaving Dad. Will you be here next time I come over?"

"I don't know."

He looked at the floor. "Were you always big?"

"No. I started growing at thirteen. By fifteen, I was six two. Maxed out at sixteen. I was thin. Started lifting when I played football."

"Hmm." Nicky thought about it.

Razor looked at him. "You're not small. Average is good. Still might have a growth spurt. Your dad is six feet, and your mom is tall for a woman. I wouldn't worry about it."

"Yeah. Anyone call you names?"

"Yeah. Sasquatch, big lug, stupid, backward-thinking Neanderthal, and other stuff."

"Really? Guys called you those things?"

"No. Women said those things. Guys don't usually mess with me anymore. Unless they've been drinking. Why? Someone calling you names?"

"Uh, yeah."

"Ignore him."

"Um, it's a girl."

"Ignore her." Then he added. "Unless you like her."

Nicky shrugged. "She's cute. She calls me a nerd. I like computers and gaming, but I'm good at sports too."

"Is that what the weightlifting is about?"

"Yeah, I guess. I mean, I want to be strong. Maybe join the military someday. But like I said, I like computers and gaming too."

"Drones and cyber are the latest things in the military. Need to be smart, like a nerd. We use drones as SEALs. They help us scout ahead and other things. I don't know much about cyber. I was a breacher, a door-kicker. But they sent me to demolition school. I can blow stuff up and crack alarms. You do what you want. You have time. You can be an athletic nerd."

"Yeah, I guess. What about the girl?"

"Next time she calls you a nerd, say thank you and give her a box of chocolates or a pretty flower. It'll throw her off. She'll either like it or leave you alone."

Nicky thought about it. "OK. Thanks, Razor. It was fun hanging out with you. I hope to see you again." He walked over and held his hand out to shake. Razor smiled, stood, and shook Nicky's hand.

"It was nice meeting you, Nicky."

Hammer appeared in the doorway. "Nicky, you ready?"

"Yeah, Dad." He swung his backpack over his shoulder. "See you, Razor. Thanks."

"Anytime."

Hammer gave a half smile as Nicky walked out and said, "Yeah, thanks, Razor." He'd heard them talking and decided to let the conversation continue. Following Nicky out, he looked at Monica, who was waiting in the kitchen. "I'll give you a call later. We need to talk. Nothing bad."

"Bye, Dad. Thanks again for the shirt," Nicky said, hugging him.

"Take care, kiddo. Love you," Hammer said, rubbing the top of his head. "Bye, Monica. Hey, uh . . . you think maybe we could have dinner sometime?"

"You can come over for dinner. Just let me know."

"No, I mean can I take you out for dinner sometime? Just us."

"Call me," she said with a slight smile. She started the vehicle and backed out of the driveway as Hammer watched.

"She didn't say no," he said to himself. Walking back inside, he found Razor drinking a beer in the kitchen. "You did good with Nicky. I heard about the girl calling him a nerd. I'll talk to Monica about it."

"I didn't overstep?"

"No. I'm glad he was comfortable enough to talk to you. You would have told me, right?"

"Yeah. Unless he said not to. But he didn't, so if you have questions—"

"Not right now. Thanks again."

"No problem. You got an ironing board and an iron?"

*****

On Monday morning, Razor put on the slacks he'd ironed the night before and the boots he'd cleaned. He pulled on the shirt, buttoned it, and tucked it into the slacks. He looked at the belt and the Texas buckle. Changing his mind, he put on the smaller regular belt instead of the one with his rodeo buckle. Going into the bathroom, he looked at himself in the mirror. Then he chickened out and changed into his cargo pants and T-shirt.

"Taking the bike out to get it inspected and registered," Razor said to Hammer, who was scrolling through his phone on the couch in the living room.

"Already? You think it'll pass?"

"Yeah."

"I need to sign the paperwork. So we can trailer it until it's legal." Hammer went to his desk in the room Razor was staying in and retrieved all the necessary paperwork, such as insurance and stuff. Outside, they hooked the trailer up to Hammer's truck. Then they loaded the bike and drove to an inspection station. It passed, just as Razor thought, so they went to the Department of Motor Vehicles to register it.

Razor looked at Hammer. "I want to run an errand. Can I take it out for a ride?"

"Sure. I'll see you later," Hammer said.

Razor put on a helmet that Hammer had brought and drove to the address he'd looked up on his phone. He rode the bike around the block and found a spot in a parking lot across the street. Sitting on the bike, he watched the building. Eve was probably out showing properties. He pretended to look at his phone every once in a while. A few people went in and out of the entrance to her business. He looked up her website again. She had a few people who worked for her. Those were probably her employees. Not wanting to draw attention to himself or have someone call the cops thinking he was acting suspicious, he decided to leave.

*****

"How did the bike do?" Hammer asked.

"Fine. Can I borrow your truck tomorrow morning?"

"Sure. Just leave me the keys to the cycle, but I don't have plans," Hammer told him.

"You don't have to go back to work?"

"I'm taking some more time off to decompress. I've learned that I need to do that every now and again."

"Good idea. You can always call me if you need to," Razor said.

"Hey, you want to go to the Rally Point tonight?" Hammer suggested.

Razor shook his head. "No. Let's wait until later in the week."

"OK."

"Uh, you got any binoculars?"

"Yeah," Hammer said suspiciously. He went to his bedroom closet, then handed the case to Razor. "Hunting or stalking?"

"Gathering intel."

*****

On Tuesday morning, Razor drove to the same parking lot. It was an hour before her real estate office opened. He watched and waited. A thought crossed his mind. *Was he stalking her?* That wasn't his intention. He just wasn't ready to approach her yet. Or was he? His hand was sweaty, and he wiped it on his pants. He was nervous thinking about her. Would she be angry with him for those drunk texts he sent her? Had she moved on? If he just went to her, those questions would be answered. He sighed. "I'd rather be in a firefight with the enemy than face her right now." *Then why am I here?* Again, he sighed, wondering why Eve drove him crazy. *I can't get you out of my mind.* His self-talk was interrupted at eight fifteen when a man unlocked the door and went inside. They didn't open until nine, so Razor figured he must be an employee. He checked the website for details and saw the man's picture and a short biography. A woman came in next, but it wasn't Eve. Administrative assistant, according to the website. Ten minutes later, he grabbed the binoculars. It was her. Eve. As stunning as ever. No, more so than when he last saw her. Dressed impeccably in a designer pantsuit. She wore her hair in a french braid. His heart skipped a beat, and butterflies fluttered in his stomach. He put the binoculars down as she went inside. He took in a slow, deep breath, then let it out. Finally seeing her from across the street in a parking lot, it felt as if no time had passed at all.

"OK, Razor. What's the plan?" he said out loud. "No point in any of this if she's serious with someone." He growled and looked at his phone.

He dialed a familiar number. "General Burke," John answered.

"Little John. Razor."

"What's up? I have meetings all day, so I can't do lunch today. Are you even in town?"

"Virginia Beach area. Question. I need to discreetly run background on someone. Uh, the last four to six months. How do I do that? She's a civilian," Razor explained.

"You can't. Hire a PI or . . . is this about a girl?" John was guessing.

"Yeah. You can't help an old buddy?"

John sighed and thought a few seconds. "What's her name?"

"Eve Patterson. Evelyn Patterson. She owns Patriots and Veterans Realty, Virginia Beach." He gave him her last known address at the condo.

"Anything specific you want to know?"

"Boyfriends or whatever."

"Did you google her?"

"Yeah."

"Did you check her social media?"

"Uh, no." Razor felt stupid for not thinking of that.

"Look there first. Then if you still need help, call me. But a background check won't say if she's got a boyfriend. You know this stuff."

"Yeah, you're right. Thanks."

John's curiosity got the best of him. "Did you see her? Sam?"

"Yeah. She's OK. Still angry with you."

"I figured."

"She said you pushed her and that she ended up in the hospital. Not cool, John." Razor made his disapproval clear.

"Andrew checked on her." Although he'd told Andrew to stay away from her, John knew he would call the hospital.

"You didn't go in person. No one did. That was wrong. No matter what."

"Hindsight is twenty-twenty. I made a mistake. I have to go. I have a meeting."

"Goodbye, John. I hope it works out." Razor pressed the red button on his phone, ending the call. Razor wasn't on social media much. He only downloaded the apps after he started therapy. It was a way for him to connect with old SEAL teammates and navy buddies. He pulled up one app and searched her name; several came up. He couldn't find one that was her. He did find her Realtor site on social media. Of course that didn't say anything about boyfriends. The other app yielded the same results. He googled her again with a different search engine, thinking it might make a difference. Nothing.

Suddenly, his phone dinged. He received a text from John: Same address. Unknown on boyfriends. That was fast.

He sent a text back: Whiskey will be forthcoming. Thx, buddy. He looked at his watch. "It's kind of scary he got that so fast," he said out loud. *I must have made him feel guilty.* He had an idea and phoned Hammer.

"Hammer, I need you to buy a house."

"What? No. I am not getting mixed up in your scheme. Just go talk to her."

Razor growled. "Not yet." He disconnected the call. His phone rang. It was Hammer.

"Look, if she finds out you're stalking her and running checks on her, she'll be pissed."

"John called you," Razor said.

"He said the same thing. Barrett runs checks on anyone her kids get serious with. She found something out about her daughter-in-law, and it caused problems later. It's OK now, but why go through that, Razor? Especially if you care about her. Just think about it. If you want me to help you, I will. But think about it."

"Finished?" Razor asked.

"Yeah."

Razor hung up just as Eve came out the door. Figuring she might be leaving, he started the truck and watched as she walked down the sidewalk to a parking lot next to her building. John and Hammer were right. He needed to confront her. But not right now. Razor drove slowly and didn't look when he passed the parking lot where Eve got into her SUV. All the way back to Hammer's place, he talked himself into going to see her. He walked in and set the keys on the hook by the door. Taking a beer from the fridge, he sat down at the kitchen table. Hammer was sitting across from him, working on his laptop.

"You're right," Razor said, taking a sip of the beer.

Hammer closed his laptop and crossed his arms. "I'm not bailing you out of jail for stalking her."

Razor narrowed his dark, bushy eyebrows.

Hammer looked at him. "Why did you ask me if I lived in Norfolk?"

"Curious."

"No. Tell me the truth." He stared at him, waiting for an answer. "You miss her and you told me you never contacted her. Except for those drunken texts." He uncrossed his arms. "This is what I see, buddy. You left your girl and went through a tough time. You went to Texas for the right reason. To help out your family. But you let things get out of hand and you were miserable. So much so that you were going to off yourself."

Razor growled. He was almost sorry he'd told Hammer that.

Hammer shook his head. "You should have called me or one of the other guys on your team. Hell, you probably could have called her."

"No. Eve has nothing to do with why I felt the way I did. The guys don't want to hear . . . I got help. I help others now. I do buddy checks. That's why we went to see Barrett. Buddy check."

"I know. Now what's your primary mission here?"

Razor sighed. "Get the girl. Or at least see if I have a chance."

"What did you find out?"

"She lives at the same address. Still has her company."

"You need to attack from the front. This mission doesn't require secrecy or stealthy, drawn-out, sneaky shit. Attack from the front and take the hits if they come. Then you'll know and can go from there." He held out his fist. "I'll be here for you, brother."

Razor relaxed his face, and his eyebrows became two again. He knew Hammer was right. He balled up his hand and bumped Hammer's fist. "Thanks, brother."

*****

That night, Razor starched and ironed his slacks and shirt again, then hung them up. He looked at his boots and wiped them off. They were his favorite boots. Full-quill ostrich that he bought as soon as he arrived back in Texas. This pair was for going out on dates or for nice occasions. He hadn't worn them very often, but he wanted to look presentable to Eve. He was nervous as he went to bed.

*****

The next morning, he took a shower and dressed after eating breakfast and drinking a cup of coffee. He was worried he might spill on his shirt, so he dressed last. He felt his beard and growled. He walked out to the kitchen, and Hammer whistled at him.

"Wow! You look great. Wait a minute. Let me trim you a little better. And you got hair on your neck. Take your shirt off."

"I'm fine."

"No. If you're going to do this, do it right. Come on." They walked to Hammer's bedroom, and Razor took off his shirt and gently laid it on the bed so it wouldn't wrinkle. Hammer came out of the master bathroom with a small hair trimmer and a towel. "Sit in the chair." Hammer trimmed his neck and his beard. When he was finished, his beard was closely cropped and neat. Then he touched it up and trimmed around Razor's ears. Satisfied with his work, he stepped back. "Looks good. You look like a movie star rather than a yeti or a sasquatch," Hammer said as he brushed the hair away.

Razor went into the bathroom and looked at himself. *This is as good as it's gonna get,* he thought. He wet a washcloth and cleaned his neck again, then exited the bathroom.

"Take the truck, and good luck. Call me if you need to."

Razor took the keys and drove to her place of business. He parked and watched. At 8:10 a.m., the man came, 8:20 a.m., the woman. He waited, and at 8:30 a.m. . . . she didn't come. At 9:00 a.m., he started the truck. Then he saw her. She looked different. She was wearing jeans and a long-sleeved shirt. Her hair was loose, and her head was down. She was wearing sunglasses. The binoculars were still in the truck, and he picked them up and tried to see into the office, but the morning glare from the sun made it difficult. *Maybe today's not a good day. No, go attack now. The worst she can say is no.*

He glanced at the bundle of flowers on the seat next to him and hesitated. Then he grabbed them and got out of the truck, checked his face in the side mirror, and looked at his reflection in the window. He popped a breath strip in his mouth and approached her office. Taking a deep breath, he opened the door and went inside. He looked around but didn't see her. She probably had her own office.

"May I help you, sir?" the woman asked, walking over.

"I'm here to see Miss Patterson."

"Um, I'm sorry. She not taking appointments today. May I be of help? Are you looking for property?" she asked but doubted it when she saw the flowers.

Eve entered the office lobby from a door at the back. "Daphne, would you handle these—" She looked up and saw him. "Zack?"

He smiled. "Hi, Eve."

Suddenly, she turned and walked briskly back into her office, closing the door. She was still wearing those sunglasses.

*****

Eve leaned against the door and swallowed. Her breathing was quick and shallow. *Why was Zack here? Why now? This couldn't have been a worse time for him to show up.* Her heart ached to go out and talk to him. But she couldn't. She went to her desk and sat down. Eve reached for a tissue and saw her hand shaking. Both of them were shaking.

"Miss Patterson." Her assistant knocked on the door.

"Yes, just a minute," Eve said, wiping her nose. She took a deep breath and removed her sunglasses. Pulling out a compact, she reapplied the makeup, especially around her eye.

*****

"You left? Why?" Hammer asked.

"She ran into her office. What was I supposed to do?"

"I don't know, barge in after her?"

Razor shook his head. "No. I . . . uh—"

"What?" Hammer knew there was more to the story.

"You know that feeling you get when the hair on your arms stands up and then the bad guys come around the corner?" Razor said.

"Yeah?"

"I sense bad guys," Razor told him.

"What do you mean?"

Razor explained what bothered him. "Sunglasses inside. Hair covering her face."

"You think someone beat her?" Hammer asked. "Come on." He grabbed the truck keys.

"What?"

"Two things I hate are people who mess with kids and people who hurt women. Let's go find out for sure."

Razor gave him directions and told him where to park. Hammer got out, but Razor stayed in the truck. "Saddle up," Hammer said, but Razor just sat there. "You chickenshit son of a bitch. Get off your ass."

"No! I'm going back home," Razor said.

"Goddamn it, Razor. What's happened to you? You fought the bad guys for twenty years, and now that you're retired, you quit? Goddamn quitter."

"No. I just—"

"You are a chickenshit quitter. You don't deserve your trident."

Razor growled. Telling him he didn't deserve his trident was one of the worst insults he could say. Razor got out of the truck and walked over to him. "Take that back."

"Chickenshit quitter who doesn't deserve his trident."

"Take it back," he growled, towering over him as he balled his hands into fists.

"Quitter."

Razor pushed him.

"You're a quitter who doesn't love her."

"I do love her!" Razor yelled, then pushed him again.

Hammer stumbled back. "Yeah, I thought so. I take it back. You're more than worthy. If you love her, we need to help her. You got help for your problem; this is just a different problem. We need to work the problem."

Razor sighed. "When did you get so smart? Let's go." Just before they arrived at the door, Razor stopped and said, "This isn't like her. I saw her shoulder throw a guy at the Rally Point. She can handle herself. She's not a weak woman who would stay with a guy who would do that."

"Well, we'll find out."

They walked into the office, and the woman, Daphne, whom he recognized from the website, came over to them. "She's not here, sir."

"Where is she?" Razor asked.

"She asked me not to tell you. You were her boyfriend, weren't you? You retired from the navy and moved to Texas."

"How do you know that?"

Daphne looked up at him. "She talked about you all the time. She was really broken up when you left."

Hammer said, "I'm checking her office."

"She's not in there," the young man said.

Hammer strode over to him. "Are you the one? Did you hit her?"

"No! I don't hit women."

"So she is being abused," Hammer confirmed.

"Yeah. It just started. She's been seeing him a couple of months. Hold on a minute." Daphne wrote something on a small notepad and tore it off. Then she wrote something on another piece and tore it off. "I told her I wouldn't tell you where she is," she said to Razor. "So this is for you." She gave Hammer one paper. "This is his information, and it's for you," she said to Razor.

"Thanks," Razor said, taking the other paper. He read the name on it. "Doug Richardson."

"Be careful. He's an attorney. And thank you," Daphne said.

"You guys need some help?" the man asked. They stared at him. "She's been a great boss. I want to help her out.

I'm a vet, and she gave me a job when I needed it and helped me get my real estate license."

"Yeah. Come on," Razor said.

"We'll take care of him first, then check on her," Hammer said.

They piled into Hammer's truck and drove to the law office. They sat outside for a minute. "What's your name?" Razor asked the man.

"Josh."

"Branch of service?"

"Air force."

Hammer and Razor shook their heads.

"PJ," he told them.

"Spec ops pararescue?" Hammer asked.

"Yeah. Busted my knee and got shot up on a mission. Medically retired. But I'll kick this guy's ass with your help." Josh was fired up now.

"Cool your jets, PJ. If he's a lawyer, we have to be careful," Hammer said.

"What are your names?" Josh asked.

"Razor and Hammer," Razor said.

"She called you Zack."

"You call me Razor," he told him, clearly making his point.

"You guys were SEALs?"

"Yeah. How did you know?" Razor asked.

"Like Daphne said, she mentioned you. I've been there longer than Daphne. We'd have lunch and talk. Purely professional, I swear." He held up his hand as if taking an oath.

Razor nodded. "What's the plan?"

"How about intimidation?" Hammer suggested. "We go in, and, Razor, you just stand there and be you. We'll tell him we're friends of hers and that he better back off."

"We can't threaten him."

"No threats. Just explain that she's not for him and that it would be in his best interests to leave her alone," Hammer said.

They agreed and walked into the building. "Remember the cameras. Might even have voice recording in his office," Hammer said. He looked at Razor. "You OK, big guy? No violence."

"Fine."

"Stay cool. Just stand there and stare at him. Josh, you take lead and do the talking. At least at first." Hammer pushed the elevator button for the fifth floor, where Richardson's office was located. Walking down the hall, they found his door and went inside.

Josh spoke. "Mr. Richardson, please."

"Do you have an appointment?" the receptionist asked.

"No."

"I'm sorry. He's booked solid today. I can fit you in tomorrow," she said, looking at her computer screen.

"Fine. What time?"

"Three? Name, please?"

"Mr. Bond," Josh said.

"OK, Mr. Bond. Tomorrow at three." The woman clearly knew they weren't clients. Not from the way they were dressed. Maybe Mr. Bond was, but not Hammer and Razor. She hesitated, then said, "He goes to lunch every day at eleven thirty at the Cheesecake Factory." She smiled at Josh and went back to work.

They left. "You think she knows and that was her way of telling us?" Josh asked.

"Maybe," Hammer said.

"I'm not waiting a day," Razor said. "We need to see her."

"I agree," Hammer said. "Let's go back to the truck and figure out what we want to do."

They waited. "We can't touch him. He'll just press charges or get a restraining order," Josh said from the back seat.

At eleven fifteen, Razor spoke up. "I'm hungry. Cheesecake Factory."

"You want to do this inside the restaurant?" Hammer asked.

"Watch him, gather intel."

Hammer smiled. "See? You came up with a plan, door-kicker," he teased. "All right." They drove the short distance to the Cheesecake Factory. Josh pointed to a specific table that gave them a view of the door and the restaurant. Josh watched the door, and Hammer and Razor scanned the other tables.

"There he is," Josh said, looking over his menu.

Hammer glanced up and saw the man Josh identified. Richardson was led to a table where Hammer had the best view of him. He undid the button on his expensive suit coat and sat down, smiling at the hostess. His server brought him a drink as if she knew what he'd order.

"Creature of habit. He already has his drink. Looks like whiskey," Hammer said. A woman walked over, and Richardson smiled and stood up. "Woman approached him." Then Hammer's face got hard as he saw Richardson kiss her on the lips and hold her chair. The server brought her a glass of wine.

"What's that look?" Razor asked, not able to see Richardson.

Hammer didn't say anything. Maybe she was just a good friend. But he watched as Richardson took her hand and rubbed the back of it with his thumb. She laughed at something he said. He was flirting.

"Hammer," Razor growled.

"He's a cheat. He's flirting with her." Hammer watched them throughout lunch.

Razor excused himself to go to the restroom. In reality, he wanted to get a look at this guy. When he came back to the table, Hammer knew he was angry.

"You need to maintain control, Razor. Focus on the mission. We're gathering intel," Hammer reminded him.

Josh paid for their lunch, but they stayed until Richardson was done. "They're leaving," Hammer said. The men departed and kept a respectable distance. Razor and Hammer knew how to follow targets. It was second nature because they'd had to do it on missions. "Razor, get the truck. I'll follow them," Hammer told him.

"Who put you in charge?" Razor asked.

Hammer said, "Sorry, buddy. I just . . . look, this is personal for you. I don't want you getting into trouble. I know I'd want to beat the shit out of that guy if he hurt my ex-wife."

Razor stared at him. Once again, Hammer was right. He was getting angrier as time went on. Thinking about that guy hitting Eve when they were in the office and now to find out he's cheating on her. "I'll get the truck."

Hammer and Josh followed them as they walked a couple of blocks and turned the corner. They went a little farther, then Richardson stopped and held open a door to a nearby building. "Shit," Hammer said as he saw the blue cloth awning over the door. "Hilton Garden Inn."

"His firm probably has a suite to entertain clients," Josh said. "He's a contract attorney, according to his website."

"Has he seen you before?" Hammer asked.

"Yeah. He's been to the office a couple of times."

"OK. Wait here. I'll follow," Hammer said. He caught up to them as they waited for the elevator. Richardson had his arm around her waist. Hammer pulled out his phone and pretended to check his email. The elevator doors opened, and Richardson and the woman walked in. Hammer followed behind and stepped into the elevator, then called Razor. He waited for Richardson to push the button for his floor. "Hey, hon. Yeah, I just got back to the hotel." Hammer pressed the button to the fifth floor, one floor above Richardson. "Yeah. It's nice. I think the kids will like the area. OK. Talk to you later." It was a ploy he'd used more than once. You pretend to be on the phone or in the middle of something so the target will push their floor button first. Or you can be polite and ask for their floor and then push yours after. Hammer hung up. Richardson and the woman got off on the fourth floor, and Hammer stayed inside. He rode to the fifth floor and then pressed the lobby button. On the way back downstairs, Hammer phoned Razor. "Pick us up in front of the Hilton Garden Inn."

Razor didn't respond to Hammer's request. He pulled the phone away from his ear when Hammer hung up. He got out of the truck and kicked one of the tires. He was angry. Taking three deep breaths, he calmed himself and climbed back into the truck. He looked at his phone and called Eve, but it went to voicemail. He started a text message: I love you and want to help. He sent it and waited. He knew she'd seen it when it said READ underneath the message. But she didn't respond. He waited a few more minutes and then picked up Josh and Hammer. Razor pulled over in a nearby lot. "What happened?" he asked them.

Hammer sighed. "He took the woman in there."

Razor growled and gripped the steering wheel so tightly that his hands and knuckles turned white, just like when he broke down in his truck. "Give me the paper," he said. Hammer stared at him. "I need to see her."

Hammer got out of the truck and opened the driver's side door. "It's my truck. I'll drive." Hammer knew Razor was angry and was having difficulty controlling it. Razor got out and went to the passenger seat. "PJ, we can take you back to work."

"I'd still like to help," Josh said.

"Give us your number, and we'll be in touch," Hammer told him. Josh gave him his card with his work and mobile numbers on it.

"Please call," Josh said as they stopped in front of the building that housed Eve's office.

They nodded and drove off. Hammer loaded the address into the GPS; fifteen minutes later they were at an apartment complex. There was a code to enter, and Hammer pressed the numbers that were written on the paper. They parked and walked up the steps to the apartment. Razor checked his phone, but Eve still hadn't responded to his text. They stood in front of the door, and Razor gave Hammer a silent nod to ask for privacy. Hammer walked down the hall and waited.

Razor knocked on the door. "Eve, it's me. Please answer." Silence. He texted her: I'm outside. Please let me see you. Nothing. She read it but didn't answer. "Eve, I came in this morning to see if you'd give me a chance. I had a rough time at home. It got really bad for a while, but things are better now. My dad passed, and my mom is living with my sister. I'm selling the property and was thinking about moving back here. I'll probably move back anyway. This is where I belong." He stopped and leaned his head against the door. "I was thinking about getting a job helping the teams. That's what my buddy Hammer is doing. Even if you don't want to get back together, I'd still like to help you. Please. No one should be hurting you, Eve. Please let me help." It was the most he'd ever said to her at one time. He touched the door and waited. He believed she was there and was listening.

*****

On the other side of the door, Eve sat on the floor, leaning against it. Her knees were pulled up to her chest, tears running down her cheeks. Her left eye was swollen, and shades of green, yellow, red, and black were starting to show. Her left wrist was also swollen and painful, and she cradled it against her body. She wanted to reach out to Zack, but she couldn't. Not yet.

*****

"I'm not leaving Norfolk until I fix this for you. I love you, Eve." Razor waited a minute and then walked down the hall toward Hammer.

"No luck?" Hammer asked.

"She was there. We need to get this guy."

CHAPTER 14

"Any ideas?" Razor asked Hammer as they went back to his truck.

"You mean other than beating the shit out of this guy?"

"Yeah. No jail," Razor said.

"She should go to the police. Get a restraining order. Pepper spray and a gun."

Razor wondered why he didn't tell her that. He texted her: I'll go to the police with you.

*****

Doug Richardson pulled his pants on and smiled at the woman in the bed. He'd met her at a party his firm had thrown for some clients. She was a paralegal in a different division of the law firm he worked for. She drove over from nearby Chesapeake, Virginia.

"Do you have to leave, Doug?" she said.

"Yes. I have to make more money so I can give you gifts like this." He pulled a box from the pocket of his suit coat and handed it to her.

"Doug." She opened it and looked at the gold necklace with a small diamond hanging from it. "It's beautiful. Thank you."

He pulled his shirt on and finished dressing, not saying anything. She took the necklace out and said, "Doug, a little help?" He sat on the bed and put it on her. He ran his hands over her shoulders. Then he kissed her. "When can we get together again?" she asked.

"I'll call you in a few days. I have some appointments out of town." He heard a ding and felt the vibration of his phone, signaling the arrival of a message. He pulled it out of his pocket and looked at it. "What the hell!" He was suddenly angry and knocked the lamp off the table.

The woman was startled and instinctively backed away. He looked at her and took a breath. "Sorry, honey. It's business," he lied. "I have to deal with idiots. I'll call you." He moved toward her, but she was trembling. "You didn't do anything wrong." He touched her bare shoulder as she held the sheet to cover her naked body. He smiled and kissed her. Then he left.

*****

He walked out of the hotel and back to his office. "Mr. Richardson, your one thirty is here," his receptionist told him.

"What else do I have?"

"The Peterson contract, and you have a meeting with the Sinclair Group."

"Shit. I'll have to deal with Peterson later. Call the Sinclair Group and see if they can come thirty minutes early, or if they can reschedule, that'd be better."

"Yes, sir."

"Send . . . whoever in."

"Yes, sir."

*****

The Sinclair Group said they'd come first thing in the morning, which meant Doug could leave early. He drove to Eve's office and walked in. "Good afternoon . . . uh, Daphne," he said, smiling at her.

"She's not here, Mr. Richardson," Daphne told him flatly.

He stopped on his way to her office, then turned and looked at Daphne. "I'll check for myself." Doug opened her door and went inside. Seeing that it was empty, he walked down a short hall to the restroom and opened the door. It was also empty. Approaching Daphne, Doug leaned on the corner of her desk. "Where is she?"

"Showing a condo out at the beach," she said.

"The beach. Why do I think you're lying to me?" he said softly as he scanned her legs. She pulled herself closer to the desk so that he could see only her skirt.

"It's on her schedule. See?" She showed him her computer screen.

"Where is this condo? No—when do you expect her back?"

"I don't. She's finished for the day after that."

Doug stood up, looking at her cleavage. He smiled, turned, and walked out.

Josh joined Daphne as she breathed a sigh of relief.

"You OK?" Josh asked.

"Yeah. He's a creep. I can't believe she got involved with him."

"Must have put on a good act in the beginning," Josh said.

*****

Eve was lying low at Daphne's apartment when her phone rang. *Doug. Oh no.*

She took in a deep breath and answered. "Where are you?" Doug asked through gritted teeth.

"Um, showing a condo."

"And then?"

"Home," she said, shaking.

"Talk to anyone today?"

"No."

"Thinking of contacting anyone? Old boyfriends or the police?"

"No." *Why would he ask that?* she wondered.

"Be home in half an hour," he demanded and hung up.

Eve looked at the time on her phone. She needed to leave now in order to get back to the condo before Doug. As soon as Razor had left the office that morning, Eve said she needed to go, but Doug knew where her condo was. Daphne had suggested she go to her apartment, so she gave her the address and the code to get inside. For those few hours, she had felt a little bit of relief. Until he called. She picked herself up off the floor and slipped on her flats, then looked for her sunglasses and keys.

*****

"Hammer." Razor nodded at the BMW SUV that drove through the gate.

"You sure?"

"Yeah, that's her," Razor told him.

Hammer followed Eve back to her condo. "This is where she lives. Third floor, balcony faces the ocean," Razor said. She pulled into a spot and slowly got out of the vehicle. "Something is wrong with her arm," he added, observing her.

"Yeah, I see the way she's holding it. Damn it." They watched as she went into the building. Hammer began to get out of truck, but Razor stopped him when he saw another vehicle arrive.

"Wait." Razor noticed Richardson pull into a parking spot a moment later. He backhanded Hammer in the chest. "He's here."

"He looks angry," Hammer said as Razor started to get out of the truck. But Hammer grabbed his arm to stop him. "Slow down, big guy. We have to be careful. Are the binoculars still here?"

"Yeah, but—"

"I feel like a walk on the beach. To look at some birds," Hammer said.

"Let's listen at the door," Razor said.

"OK. We'll walk by the door and listen for a bit. But I don't want some nosy neighbor calling the cops on us. We'll take the binocs just in case we have to relocate to the beach."

"Fine." As they walked to the building, Razor said, "I just don't get it. She's a strong, independent woman. She wouldn't put up with that shit."

Hammer stopped. "I had a teacher in high school. She was nice and a really good teacher. One day she came in wearing long sleeves in May. It was hot, and the school was always comfortable. Then she came in with a broken arm. Then we had a substitute the final week of school. Her husband beat her to death because she wouldn't stop grading papers long enough to cook his dinner. Her friend tried to get her to leave him, but she said he promised to stop. It never stops." He paused. "It haunts my mom to this day. She wished she'd done more to help."

*****

Doug had made a copy of her condo key without asking. She listened as he placed it in the door and opened it. As he walked in, she heard the keys rattle before he returned them to his pants pocket. "Get out here!" he yelled.

She came out of the bedroom and looked at him. She'd found an ACE bandage and had wrapped her wrist. Walking to the kitchen, she poured herself a glass of whiskey.

He followed, and she could feel his eyes on her. "Where were you?"

"Showing a condo."

"Bullshit."

"Believe what you want," she said, taking a sip of her drink.

He scoffed at her. She walked out to the living area and then to the balcony. She took a deep breath and thought about Razor and that time in the ocean. She was shaking as he came up behind her. She knew he could push her over the rail. She might break something and live, or she might land in a way that would kill her. It was a toss-up. She took another sip of her drink.

As if reading her mind he looked at the ground below them. "You'd probably break your back and be in a wheelchair.

Of course, then I could screw you without much of a fight. But I won't be changing your diapers, so get that thought out of your head," he said. She cringed as he ran a hand up her back. "What's for dinner? Can't go out now." He placed a finger under her chin and turned her head so that he could see her eye. "You should be more careful." He moved his hand to the back of her neck and squeezed slightly. "I asked you what was for dinner."

"I'll need to see what I have." As she spoke, she saw a man on the beach turn and look toward her. It wasn't Zack, but he reminded her of him. He had a beard and appeared to be military or ex-military. Virginia Beach had a lot of those types in the area. The man took his shirt off and sat down in the sand, presumably to look at some sailboats with his binoculars.

"Get on it. I had a workout after lunch, and I'm hungry." He smirked.

"You mean you screwed your new girlfriend," she said, knowing what would happen if she called him out.

He grabbed her hair and pulled her head back. "You'll pay for that comment later," he whispered. Then he smiled and kissed her hard on the lips. "Fix dinner, sweetheart." He let her go and went inside. He sat on the couch and turned the TV on. *"Now!"* he yelled.

She saw the man on the beach turn and glance at her again, but this time he brought the binoculars up and quickly looked. Then he put them down and waved. *He might be a friend of Zack's.* She smiled and moved her hand in front of her body in a quick return gesture and then went back inside the condo.

*****

Eve fixed chicken breasts and some vegetables.

They were eating at the table when he asked, "Who has been texting you?"

"What? No one. Clients."

"Who is texting you?" he asked again, slowly, as his anger grew.

"Clients and my employees," she told him.

He set his fork down and took out his phone. He pulled up an app and read the texts she had received on her phone: "I love you and want to help. I'm outside. Please let me see you. I'll go to the police with you." He stared at her. "Now, are you going to continue to lie to me?"

"Are you spying on me? Using your contacts at the police department?"

He laughed. "Technology makes it easy today. This app is so that parents can see who their kids are texting. But it works fine for my purposes." He stared at her. His cruel eyes seemed to grow darker as his anger rose to the surface and his face turned red. "You lied to me. I don't like that. Since you've shown me you can't be trusted, I'll need to take your phone. Just like a child, you must be punished."

"I need my phone for work."

"Clients can reach you at the office. There was life before cell phones. Give it to me. I won't ask again." His jaw was clenched, and she knew he was going to explode.

She reached into her pocket and passed him the phone with shaking hands. Her lifeline. He was taking a lifeline away from her. "I didn't respond to him. It's not my fault. I don't know who it is, so it must be a mistake. Please, Doug."

His dark eyes bore a hole in her undamaged one, and she broke contact. "Yes, it would have been worse if you had responded. But *Zack* has your number." He placed the phone in front of her face to unlock it. She watched as he searched her contacts, presumably looking for Zack. He sighed. "You lied again. He's in your contact list. In fact, he's a favorite." Doug slapped her across the face. "Tell me who he is."

"He's . . . just an old . . . friend. He moved away." Eve held her cheek.

"Hmm. Seems like he might be back in town." Doug drummed his fingers on the table as he thought.

Eve watched as he typed with his thumbs.

"There. I told him this was the wrong number. Hopefully, that will work. I was going to give you a chance to earn your phone back, but I don't think so." He picked up his fork and finished eating. "I suppose I'll have to change my tactics now."

"What does that mean?" she asked.

"I'll have to be nicer while he's in town. Or at least not leave visible . . ." He trailed off. She got his point. "Hopefully, that won't be for long." He stood, and Eve watched him as went back to the couch and found a baseball game on the television. "Bring me a drink."

She got up and went to the door. He shot out of his seat and grabbed her arm. "What do you think you're doing?"

"Going out to get the mail."

He laughed. He pushed her to the side, then put the chain on the door and turned the dead bolt. "No, you aren't. Now get me a drink. Whiskey."

She walked back to the kitchen and poured a glass of whiskey for herself and downed it. In another glass, she poured him one, then placed it on the coffee table. She turned and went back to the kitchen table to clear it and take care of the dishes.

*****

Eve was sitting in the bedroom when he yelled for her. "Eve!" She sighed and went to the living room. "Bring me another drink, honey." She got the bottle and set it on the coffee table. "Have a drink with me. Come sit down. We can watch a movie."

"I'm tired," she told him.

"I'm trying to be nice."

She retrieved her glass from the kitchen and poured a healthy amount. She sat on the couch.

"Come on, closer." He patted the spot next to him. She moved nearer to him, and he put his arm around her. "That's better." He found an action movie.

After a few more glasses of whiskey, he took her hand and set it on his leg. He moved it up to his groin and began rubbing himself against it.

"Stop it, please," she said, pulling her hand away. "You can go out. Go see her."

He laughed. "You're giving me permission to go get laid." He laughed again. "That's funny. I'm here and you're here now. Besides, you were a bad girl today. I haven't forgotten about that comment you made or about the texts."

"The texts weren't my fault. I didn't even text back."

"You lied to me. Twice."

"What happened to you? You were such a nice guy. But that was all an act, wasn't it?" she said.

"I can be nice." But he said it sarcastically. He grabbed her hand again, leaned over, and touched her cheek with his other hand. Then he closed the space and gently kissed her. "See. Nice." He kissed her neck, then turned back to the movie.

There was a knock on the door. "Police. Open the door."

"What the hell? Well, I know you didn't call them. Don't move from that couch, and don't try anything." He got up and went to the door. Opening it, he smiled. "Officers, what can I do for you?"

"We had a report of loud noises, yelling, and fighting."

"We didn't hear anything, and it wasn't us. We're watching a movie, right, hon?" He glanced at Eve. Then he stepped out with them. "I'm Doug Richardson. Is Captain Driscoll on duty tonight?"

"No," the officer said. "Sir, may we come inside and speak to you?"

"Look, it's probably some kids pranking you guys. You know, that new thing called swatting. All is quiet. Let me make a call." He phoned Driscoll. "Hey, Kurt. Doug here. I think some kids were messing with your officers and called in a noise complaint. Yeah." Doug handed his phone to one of the officers.

"Yes, sir. Yes, but . . . yes, sir." He returned Doug's phone. "Sorry to bother you, sir." The officers left, and Doug watched them from the doorway.

When they were out of sight, he secured the dead bolt and replaced the chain. He smirked and sat back down.

Eve began to stand up. "Where are you going?" he asked, yanking her down.

"Can't I go to the bathroom?"

Another slap left a stinging sensation on her already red cheek.

"Don't talk back to me. Go."

Eve went to the bathroom in her bedroom and locked the door. She splashed water on her face as she leaned over the sink. "Zack, I'm sorry. I've made a mistake," she said quietly and began to cry. She unwrapped her wrist and took a shower. The water felt good as she let it flow over her body. She still felt the sting of his hand on her face, and her wrist hurt, but she was at peace for those twenty minutes.

Eventually, Doug banged on the door, startling her. "Hurry up!"

Turning the water off, she stepped out and dried herself. She avoided looking in the mirror at first, then saw her face. A black eye and a red cheek. She rewrapped her swollen wrist and dressed. She brushed her wet hair and dried it, taking her time. After finishing her nighttime routine, she came out of the bathroom.

He was sitting on the edge of the bed. "You shower in the mornings. Why the change?"

"I just . . . I don't know. I wanted a shower."

He scowled at her. She looked like a teenager in the paisley sleep shorts and purple T-shirt with Hello Kitty on it. "What the hell are you wearing?"

"Pajamas. I thought they were cute. Are you going to criticize what I wear now?"

"You just don't learn, do you?" He stood up. Walking over to her, he sighed. Without warning, he punched her in the stomach. She doubled over and gasped. "That was for the comment about my girlfriend." He grabbed her arm, pulled her up, and then punched her again. This time, she went down to her knees, and he knocked her over. She coughed, holding her stomach. "That was for lying to me." He kicked her in the stomach. Her arms were in the way, and she yelled when his shoe made contact with her injured wrist. He walked off while she lay on the floor, coughing and crying.

He returned holding scissors, then pulled her to her feet. "Stand up." He took the scissors and cut the pajama shirt up the middle and ripped it off her. He moved the scissors to her shorts and cut them up one side and then the other. He nicked her thigh, and she began to bleed a little. "Oops," he said, laughing. She stood in just her underwear. His face went cold. "You aren't twelve. Don't dress like it." He went to the bathroom and slammed the door.

Eve slowly made her way over to the dresser, holding her stomach. She found a short nightgown and carefully put it on. No. She needed to leave now. She walked to the bedroom door and reached for the knob, but it was different. It had a keyhole like a front door. She tried to turn it, but it was locked.

"No." She kept trying, but it was no use. He must have changed it when she was in the shower. Realizing that attempting to escape was futile, she crawled into bed and curled up, continuing to cry quietly.

When Doug came out of the bathroom, she watched him nervously. He looked at her and glanced at the door. Smiling, he said, "Did you check the door?" Eve was silent. "Of course you did. I'd expect nothing less. Always one step ahead. I learned from my mistakes. I won't make those again."

Mistakes. He won't make them again, Eve thought, closing her eyes. She opened them again. "Have you done this before?" she asked, not moving.

He ignored her question and crawled into bed, then kissed her on the shoulder. "Good night, sweetheart."

All she could do was close her eyes and silently pray.

*****

She woke to him kissing her on the neck. "Stop. Doug. Please."

"Shut up."

"Doug, no."

"I said shut up, or I'll make you. Just lay there."

"I'm saying no. You do this, and you're a rapist."

He lifted his head and laughed. "Wouldn't be the first time. Don't make me do something you'll regret."

"I regret the day I met you." She spit in his face.

Kimberly A. Biggerstaff © 2025

He slapped her and grabbed her by the neck, strangling her. He moved over her as she struggled to breathe. He kept one hand on her throat and moved the other down to her panties. She hit him and tried to pry his hand from her neck. He loosened his grip and let go as she gasped and took a breath. He tore the nightgown off her, then pulled her panties off.

She hit him in the chest and tried to push him off, but she couldn't. "Stop fighting," he said. "You know you want it." He held her arms down, and she spit at him again. "You goddamn bitch." He began to strangle her again. She fought him with all the strength she had left until she finally passed out.

*****

She woke when he put smelling salts under her nose. Then he did what he wanted. She couldn't fight. She could barely move. Her body hurt as a tear ran down from her eye.

CHAPTER 15

Razor had stayed at the door listening for most of the night. Eventually, he gave up and walked downstairs to Hammer's truck, where he was waiting inside.

Razor opened the passenger door and got in. "I didn't hear anything but mumbling," he told him. "I think they're in the bedroom." He looked at his watch.

"I saw her from the beach. She knows we're here."

"We can't stay here. Police might come back and arrest the wrong guys."

"She'll have to hang on and get through tonight," Hammer said.

"What happened when you talked to the cops?" Razor asked. When the police had arrived earlier, Razor had enough time to run downstairs and head toward the beach. Then he and Hammer walked back to the truck. They waited, and when the police left, Hammer approached them. Razor wanted to see if he could hear anything and went back up to Eve's door, watching and listening.

"I told them my wife and I were thinking about buying a condo and wondered about the safety of the area," Hammer said.

"And?"

"They said they got a noise complaint but that it was probably just kids calling it in. It's a relatively safe area."

Razor growled.

"He might have friends on the force," Hammer said. "We need a plan." They stuck around until it started to get really late, then Hammer sighed. "I hate to leave, but this isn't doing any good. He's spending the night. We'll start fresh in the morning."

Reluctantly, Razor agreed. *Hang in there, Eve. We'll figure something out.*

CHAPTER 16

Eve heard Doug as he woke early, then took a shower and dressed for work. "Wake up, Eve."

She opened her eyes, and the pain overcame her.

"I texted what's her name . . . Daphne, that you're sick and won't be in for a couple of days."

"I have—" She tried to talk. Her throat hurt and sounded raspy.

"You don't have anything. There are snacks and some food over there. Get water from the tap. And your clothes are out there." He nodded toward the bedroom door. "You won't need them today." He finished tying his tie.

She looked around the room and saw the open dresser drawers. Her closet door was also open, and she didn't see any clothes in there. Not even his.

"What? You can't leave me like this," she said in her raspy voice.

"I can do what I want. You need to learn your place and how to respect me. I'll be back this evening." He stared at her. "I'll know if you try to leave this room. I've installed some cameras, and I will find you and . . ." He stopped just short of the threat. "Just don't try to leave." He pulled the sheet away and looked at her naked body. Her torso was bruised, and there was some blood on the sheets. "What's that from? Is it that time of the month?"

She looked down and quietly said, "No."

He seemed to realize he had gotten so rough that he made her bleed. He just looked at her blankly. "Don't move." He walked out and came back with clean sheets. "Change them. Wait, no. Give me the sheets." When she didn't move, he demanded, "Give me the sheets and stuff!" He grabbed her by the arm and yanked her up. Eve pulled the sheets and comforter off the bed and handed them to him.

"There's no reason for this," she whispered.

"There's a reason for everything." He threw the linens in the hall in the pile with her clothes and walked over to her. He touched her hair with one hand and felt her breast with the other. He kissed her. But she bit him on the lip. He pushed her away. "Bitch." He slapped her and threw her on the bed. The anger inside him seeped out as he touched his lip and saw the small amount of blood. Another time and he might have been turned on. Not now. He glared at her as she looked up at him. "I don't have time for your shit. But you need another lesson."

He took his belt off and folded it in half. Turning her over, Doug swung it on her back. She cried out. He hit her again and again until her back was raw and stinging. "It's interesting how much the body and mind can take." Doug stood over her, admiring his work. He reached for her and lightly touched her back, tracing the red marks. Eve trembled as she waited for more. "I don't want you to scar, not yet. That is, if I keep you around long enough." He lowered his voice. "You may take longer to break than her." He was quiet for a moment as he silently thought about his next move. "I may need to move you sooner than I expected. But first things first."

She heard him unzip his pants, and she started to turn over, but then she felt a punch and heard a cracking noise. The pain in her side made her yell, and he quickly put his hand over her mouth. He leaned close to her ear. "Might have broken a rib on that one. Sorry about that. You really need to behave." Placing her on her stomach, he leaned over her and said, "I will break you and teach you respect."

She lay there, helpless, as he held her arms above her head on the bed. "You are a whore. A fucking tramp and a slut. You're a nobody," he told her as he forced himself on her.

*****

"You better be on the fucking pill," he said as he smiled and zipped his pants. She lay there, not moving. "Hey. Don't die on me yet." He grabbed her by the hair and yanked her head back. She moaned, and he dropped her. "You're a mess." Again, he stared at her and thought aloud. "I might have made a mistake with you. The other one was young. She was teachable. You're older. Might be set in your ways. Hmm." His eyes moved slowly over her body. "God, you are lovely. It's such a shame." Then his voice softened and changed. He sat next to her on the bed. Eve was still on her stomach, trembling, eyes closed. She heard him sigh. "Who did this to you, Eve? You did. The choices we make have consequences." He touched her back with his fingertips. He could feel her body shaking with his touch. "Don't be scared. I'll take care of you," he said in a loving, caring manner. "He gets angry. You can't make him angry, Eve." He stood and went to the bathroom. Eve heard him making noises as if looking for something. He came back and opened a jar.

"Do you want my help?"

"Doug?" she squeaked.

"Yes, baby? This is a salve. It will help and make you feel better." He placed a latex glove on his hand and then gently rubbed the salve on her back. "It feels good, doesn't it? It has healing properties, and . . . well, you'll feel better. I don't want to spoil the surprise." Doug replaced the lid and put the jar back in the bathroom. Throwing the latex glove in the trash, he washed his hands. He looked at himself in the mirror and smiled. Returning to the bedroom, he grabbed his suit jacket.

He checked his watch, and when he spoke, his voice was back to normal, deep and rough. "I have a meeting this morning. Get yourself cleaned up before I get home. Have a good day." She heard him lock the door behind him. Eve curled into the fetal position and cried.

She didn't understand how or why he had escalated so fast. No, she hadn't made it easy on herself. She'd made comments and said some things she shouldn't have. But he had gone from zero to sixty in a day. She had to get out.

Eve tried to push herself up. Slowly, she sat up and then stood. She was beginning to feel strange. Almost dizzy. The salve. What was it? She stumbled to the bathroom and tried to find the jar. She couldn't focus. Everything looked strange. Colors seemed brighter. Eve turned toward the shower. *Get it off. I need to get it off.* Stepping inside, Eve grasped the knob and turned it with both hands. Her legs felt weak. She reached for the loofah that was on a stick and pulled it off its hanger. Falling to the floor as the water ran over her, she held the stick and scrubbed her back. She grimaced in pain as she tried to get the salve off. She pressed hard as she moved it across her raw skin. Soap or shampoo. Something. She saw a bottle on the built-in shelf and pulled it. It fell, and Eve picked it up. Pressing the pump multiple times, the liquid flowed onto the loofah. Then she began to scrub her back again. She let the tears flow as she continued. Her nerve endings were on fire, but she kept scrubbing, reaching all over her back. She stopped only when the water around her began to turn pink and then red. Blood. She hoped she had gotten it off.

*****

Razor had been a nervous wreck the entire night. He didn't want to leave her. Hammer tried to calm him, but it was difficult.

"She's in trouble, Hammer. I know it," Razor said on the drive back to Hammer's house.

"We'll go back in the morning and see if she goes to work."

"I don't like this."

"You need to think of this as a mission. Leave your emotions at the door. We don't have any evidence. We need more."

"He's beating her."

"You weren't sure. She was wearing sunglasses and holding her wrist. I think that's circumstantial evidence. It's not enough."

"I won't let her die, Hammer. I can't." He looked out the passenger window, not wanting his friend to see his eyes. "I love her."

*****

Razor barely slept. All he thought about was Eve and what Doug was doing to her. Sitting up in bed, he reached for his phone. He scrolled through his contacts and pressed send.

"What the hell, Razor? It's late . . . or early. Damn, it's two in the morning."

"I'm sorry. I didn't know who to call, John. I need your help again."

"Can't this wait?"

"No. It's my girl. She's in trouble. Please."

John could hear it in his voice. He was worried. "What do you need?"

"Doug Richardson. Any information. He's an attorney in Virginia Beach." Razor told him everything he knew.

"Is there something specific you're looking for?"

"Yeah. Criminal activity. Domestic disturbances or domestic violence. Anything like that."

John stopped writing. "Who is he, Razor? Her boyfriend? Is he hitting her?"

Razor swallowed. "We think so. We need evidence. She's hiding, or he's got her so scared she won't let me help her. Please, John."

"Is Hammer with you?"

"Yes."

"Good. He'll keep you straight. Listen to him. I'll get on this right away."

"I owe you, John. Anything you need or want."

"Forget it. I'll be in touch," John said, then hung up.

An hour later, Razor's phone rang. It was John.

*****

"Hammer, let's go," Razor said.

"All right. Settle down. I told you to check your emotions."

Razor grabbed him by the shirt. "Could you check your emotions if it was Monica? Or Nicky?"

"No. But I'd rely on you to keep me from doing something stupid," Hammer said as they stared at each other.

Razor let him go. "Sorry. I have new intel."

"What new intel?"

"I called Little John, and his . . . Sam's wife ran background on Richardson."

"What came up?"

"He was briefly interviewed when an old girlfriend turned up dead. But they ruled him out."

"Anything else?"

"Yeah. They did a deep dive into his childhood. Richardson's mother burned the house down with him and a man inside. The man was his father, but they weren't married. Multiple responses to the house by police for domestic disturbances. His mother and his father died in the fire. He was seventeen."

"Was he abused?"

"They couldn't find anything. But maybe he witnessed his father beating his mother."

Hammer went to the pantry and grabbed a box of Pop-Tarts and then four bottles of water from the fridge. "Let's go."

*****

Hammer and Razor drove to Eve's office. "Is she in?" Razor asked Daphne.

"I'm glad you're here. I got a text saying she's sick and won't be in for a couple of days," she told them. "I'm worried. She doesn't text me for things like that. She would have called and given me instructions for her appointments."

"He probably took her phone," Hammer said.

Razor took out his phone and texted Eve right away. Moments later, he got a reply. Razor sighed. "He has her phone. I got another reply saying it wasn't her number." His face tightened as he clenched his jaw. "No more." He turned and left the office. Hammer ran after him.

"Hey! Slow down, Razor," Hammer called. Josh ran after them. "Razor!" Hammer repeated.

Razor stopped at the truck. "Give me the keys. You don't have to go. You have a family."

"Where are you going?" Hammer asked.

"Her place. Make sure she's not . . . I won't be a day late to save her."

"OK. Never go into a firefight without your battle buddy. I'm driving," Hammer said. "You coming, Josh?"

"Uh, no. I'll go keep an eye on Richardson. Make sure he's at his office and doesn't skip town," Josh said.

Kimberly A. Biggerstaff © 2025

"Good idea," Hammer told him. "I'll text you our numbers. Call if there's trouble."

Hammer and Razor drove to the condo and stood outside her door. Razor knocked and rang the bell. No answer. He knocked harder. *"Eve!"*

*****

She heard something but couldn't move. Her body ached and hurt. Slowly, Eve opened her eyes. She was still on the shower floor. The water had stopped running. *Did I turn it off? I must have.* Crawling out of the shower, she went to the linen closet. Looking up at it, she wasn't surprised. It was empty. No towels or sheets. Nothing. Naked, she crawled out to the bedroom. The room was dark. *Is it night already? How long was I out?* Eve went to the nightstand to turn the lamp on. She saw the time on the clock: 9:30 a.m. She looked at the windows, but they were covered by wooden boards. *When did he do that?* She didn't remember hearing any hammering. *What day is it? What . . . is that someone at the door?* She tried to yell, but her throat hurt. Eve attempted to stand, but she was tired and her back hurt, along with her stomach and ribs. She slowly crawled to the bedroom door. "Help me, please," she whispered.

*****

"Eve!" Razor yelled.

Out of nowhere, two armed police officers approached them from behind. "Sir, step away from the door," one said, his hand on his taser.

"We heard a woman yell in there," Hammer said.

"No, I don't think you did."

"We can explain, officers. No trouble from us," Hammer said.

Razor heard Eve's voice from inside. It was faint but unmistakable. "That was her."

"I didn't hear anything," the second officer said.

"I did," Razor said and kicked the door in. *"Eve!"* he yelled as he ran inside and looked for her.

"Freeze!" an officer yelled. "Taser, taser, taser!"

Hammer ran in behind him, then suddenly stiffened and fell to the ground as the eerie sound of electricity filled the room. Razor quickly went to the bedroom. *"Eve!"* He tried the door, but it was locked. He heard her make a noise and said, "Back away." Just as he kicked it open, he felt the prongs in his back and the electricity coursing through his body. Falling forward, he landed on the ground with a thud. Razor growled and tried to get up when the sound stopped, but the officer pulled the trigger again, and another burst of electricity flowed through his body.

"Stay down!" the officer yelled.

Lying on his stomach, Razor's eyes met Eve's. "Love . . . you," he managed when the electricity stopped.

"Oh my God. Call an ambulance, Tom," the officer said when he saw Eve, battered, bruised, and naked.

With her last ounce of strength, she crawled toward Razor, putting her hand on his face. "Love you too," she was barely able to say.

CHAPTER 17

Doug answered his cell phone. "Hello."

"Doug, it's Kurt. Get out of town. The police are on their way."

"What are you talking about?"

"They found her. I can't help you." He disconnected the call.

"Son of a bitch." He opened his desk drawer and grabbed his handgun, putting it in his waistband. He went to his wall safe and put all the money from there into a backpack. He walked out of his office without saying anything.

"Sir, you have . . . ," his secretary said. But he was gone. He took the elevator down and walked to his car.

"Where you going, dirtbag?" Josh asked, pulling Doug around the corner of the building. He held a gun on him.

"What the fuck are you doing? Wait, you're . . . you work for her. What do you want?"

"Citizen's arrest," Josh said.

"Yeah, right. Good luck with that." Doug kept walking.

Josh reached for him, and Doug swung around. He knocked the gun from Josh's hand and kicked him in his bad knee. Josh went down, holding his knee. "Well, that was easy," Doug said, picking up Josh's gun.

"Freeze! FBI!" yelled a female voice from behind Doug.

Doug turned and saw Daphne standing a few yards away with a gun pointed at him. She was wearing a windbreaker with FBI in yellow letters on it, and her badge hung from a chain around her neck.

"You've got to be kidding me," Doug said, laughing. "Nice costume."

"I'm arresting you on suspicion of assault, kidnapping, and . . . whatever else. Drop the weapon," Daphne said.

With a smug look on his face, Doug said, "I don't think so. I think I'll shoot him. Then shoot you. Lover's quarrel. Oh, murder-suicide. Yeah." Doug looked at Josh, who was still on the ground, then at Daphne, and fired his weapon at Josh.

"No!" Daphne yelled.

"One down." He turned the gun on Daphne, but she fired first. Doug had a look of shock on his face and fell backward as the blood soaked through his shirt. Daphne heard a noise and spun around. She saw Razor holding a gun. He lowered it as Daphne went over and kicked the gun away from Doug. She knelt to check his pulse with her left hand, and suddenly he grabbed her arm. With the other hand, he lifted a knife, but Razor fired once into his chest and one more into his forehead. He dropped the knife, and Daphne fell back, stunned.

"You OK?" Razor asked, quickly leaning down and helping her up. He kicked the knife away and knelt to make sure Doug was dead, although with a bullet in the forehead, it was unnecessary.

She nodded. "Yeah, I'm OK." Regaining her senses, she did a quick pat down and found the gun in Doug's waistband. She carefully put the weapon in her jacket pocket and went over to Josh.

"Josh, please, no." She didn't see any blood and checked his chest. Tearing his shirt open, she saw a vest. A tactical vest with a plate in it.

He coughed and looked at her. "Damn it, that hurt." He coughed again.

"What the hell, Josh?" Daphne said, surprised.

"Something . . . I learned from my PJ days. Be . . . prepared for anything." After another coughing fit, he asked, "You're FBI?"

"Yeah," Daphne said, looking down at him.

He waved her closer. "Will you . . . go to dinner . . . with me?" He smiled up at her.

"What? Yes, but first there are pressing matters to attend to." She took out her phone and called an ambulance and the local FBI office. She looked up and saw Razor standing over Doug's body.

Razor glared into Doug's cold, dark, lifeless eyes. There was no emotion. He felt empty. Nothing. Like so many times before when he killed the enemy. The only difference was that this was in the United States and he had killed an American. No. He couldn't think of it like that. He killed a bad guy. One less bad guy in this world.

CHAPTER 18

Daphne ran into the hospital room with Razor right behind her. "Eve, I'm so sorry." She went straight to her and hugged her gently as Eve winced. When Daphne released her, she looked at Eve's face. "I . . . this shouldn't have happened."

"I was an informant and knew the risks. Just tell me you got him." Daphne's face dropped, and Eve said, "No. He got away?"

"No. We had to shoot him. He's dead."

Razor growled. "Death was the easy way out."

"What do you mean, *we* had to shoot him?" Eve asked.

"My first time shooting someone," Daphne said. "But he shot Josh and turned the weapon on me. I shot him, but he wasn't dead. He was going to stab me, but Razor put two rounds into him. He'll never hurt anyone again." She looked at Razor. "You saved my life. Thank you."

Razor nodded.

"Where's Josh?" Eve asked, worried.

"Down the hall. He'll be OK. Broke his leg and bruised his chest. He was wearing body armor."

"Smart kid," Razor said.

Hammer knocked and came in. "Well, nothing like starting the day being tased, right, Razor?" he asked.

"I was tased twice," Razor said.

"Damn. You win."

Razor huffed. "It was a drinking game. Been tased a lot."

Hammer shook his head. "Is that why you were able to escape the paramedics and steal my truck?"

Razor shrugged.

"You guys got tasered?" Daphne asked.

"Wait. You're FBI?" Hammer had noticed her jacket and badge.

"Uh, yeah. I've been on this case for a while."

"What case?" Razor asked. "His old girlfriend?"

"Yes. How do you know that?"

Razor didn't say anything, but Hammer did. "We have an anonymous source." No point in getting John in trouble.

"I'll ignore that, and you should keep that to yourself." Daphne began telling the story. "About a year ago, a woman was found in the woods just south of Wakefield. She was burned, and DNA was scarce. We knew she was dating someone, but he was cleared and then disappeared. It was Richardson. I played a hunch, and it led me here to him. But I didn't have any evidence."

"That's when she approached me," Eve said. "I had been on two dates with him. She came to warn me off, but I wanted to help."

"Why didn't you arrest him after he gave her a black eye?" Hammer asked.

"I told her it was too soon," Eve said. "I wanted her to have more evidence. I was hoping he'd confess or mention the other woman. He didn't exactly confess, but he said some incriminating things."

Daphne took her hand, shaking her head. "I never meant for you to . . . Eve, you should have stopped and come to me."

"He escalated faster than I thought. I was going to contact you, but he took my phone and kept me in the condo."

"What was the hunch?" Hammer was curious about what led Daphne to Virginia Beach.

"Spouses and significant others are ruled out first. A year had passed between the time she'd been killed and found. Richardson moved here from Wakefield and joined that firm. Someone from the local police department interviewed him, but nothing came of it. I watched a copy of the interview later. At the end, he pulled out his keys, and I noticed his key chain. When I froze the tape and enlarged the image, I saw it." She showed them a photo on her phone of a close-up of a key chain. Hanging off it was a plastic piece of bread with peanut butter and jelly on it in the shape of a heart.

"What is that? A peanut butter and jelly heart?" Hammer asked.

Daphne pulled out her key chain. It had a piece of bread with a peanut butter and jelly heart. "We also interviewed her best friend. They'd been friends since high school. I did a follow-up interview with her, and she gave me this key chain. I told her I'd return this one and the other one when we got him. I can do that now, thanks to all of you."

"Good," Razor said.

"Yeah, closure is good. You got him," Hammer said.

"With your help. All of you. I can't thank you enough," she said. "Eve, I'll be back. I need to check on a certain real estate agent."

Razor stared at Hammer. "Oh, uh, yeah. I think I'll get something to drink," Hammer said, following Daphne out.

Eve reached for Razor's hand. "I heard every word you said outside Daphne's apartment. I think that's the most you've ever spoken. I'm sorry about your father. And I'm sorry about whatever it was you went through. Maybe someday we can talk about it." She smiled. "I'm glad you're here, Zack. I missed you."

"I missed you too." He kissed the back of her hand. Then he felt the need to apologize. "I'm sorry about the texts I sent you from Texas. It's not an excuse, but I was drunk when I sent them. I . . . uh . . . and there was a bull that was pissing me off."

"A bull?"

"Yeah. This one." He pulled out his phone and showed her a picture of the animal. He found the photos while he was in the VA hospital. He'd taken them one night when he was drunk. He just couldn't delete them.

"You called me that night. After the texts. No message, though."

"No. I didn't know what to say. I never got the chance to call back. I'm sorry. I would have been there for you, Zack."

"It's OK. I needed to hit rock bottom to come back." He squeezed her hand. He wanted to kiss her, but after all she'd been through, he wasn't sure. He didn't know the details, but he remembered the policeman placing a sheet over her body before the ambulance arrived. Razor knew that if she wanted to talk about it, she would. He also knew that Eve had a long recovery ahead of her. From experience, he knew the physical injuries would heal with time. It was the emotional ones that would linger. But he would be there for her, if she wanted. "Eve?"

"Yes?"

Razor grinned. "I need a Realtor. I think I'm moving back to the area."

EPILOGUE

Four years later

Razor and Eve's home, Virginia Beach

"Zack, they'll be here soon," Eve said.

"I'm ready," Razor said as the two-year-old boy ran behind him. Razor stopped, and the boy grabbed his leg and sat on his foot. "Oh, have you seen my son? Wyatt!" The boy laughed as Razor walked with him hanging on to his pant leg and sitting on his foot. "Wyatt!"

"Daddy!" the boy called from Razor's foot.

"Did you hear something?" Razor asked Eve.

She smiled. "Something is attached to your leg."

"Knock, knock," Monica said, entering through the side door and carrying a baby on her hip.

"Hey there, Mon. How's the little one?" Eve asked, tickling the baby girl.

"Good. She's crawling, and Hammer's babyproofed everything in the house—and I mean everything." Monica laughed.

"Hi, Razor!" Nicky said, fist-bumping him.

"Nicky."

"Traveling with babies is a pain in the . . . you know what," Hammer said, carrying the diaper bag and another backpack. He dropped them in the living room. "I left the portable crib in the SUV."

Razor walked over from the kitchen and handed him a beer. "It's been a few years since Nicky. You're old."

"Thanks. You're no spring chicken either. Where's my godson, Wyatt?" Hammer asked.

"I don't know." Razor shrugged.

"Uncle Nick!" Wyatt said, laughing.

"Did you hear something?" Hammer asked.

"Been hearing things all day."

"Daddy!" Wyatt called from below.

"Oh, you have a growth on your leg. Looks serious. You may have to cut that off."

Razor looked down, grabbed Wyatt, and picked him up. *"Grrr!"* Razor threw him over his shoulder and then set down the boy, who took off to find Nicky.

Hammer smiled as he watched the two-year-old run away. "Must be nice being married to a Realtor. House on the beach."

"Yeah. I can't even complain about the stairs. That elevator has come in handy. I had a generator installed if we lose power."

"You need another kid to fill one of the bedrooms," Hammer said as he looked around the large open living room. It was a modern interior with a coastal feel. Four floors with patios overlooking the ocean.

"Not yet."

*****

The patio out back had an outdoor kitchen, and the men cooked hamburgers and hot dogs on the grill. Hammer placed the burgers and dogs on plates and took them over to the patio table. Nicky and Wyatt were playing in the pool as Monica and Eve sat on the edge, keeping an eye on them.

"Time to eat!" Razor called.

Eve pulled Wyatt out of the water and took him to the patio table as Nicky and Monica joined them. Monica placed five-month-old Paige in a high chair. Razor went to a small refrigerator nearby and retrieved two more beers and a bottle of wine and a glass.

"Oh, I miss having a glass of wine," Monica said. "Still nursing."

Razor went to pour Eve a glass, but she stopped him by placing her hand over it. "Um, no. I can't."

"Why not?" Razor asked.

Eve smiled, giving him time to think about it.

Monica and Hammer looked at each other, catching on a little quicker. "*Hoorah!* Congratulations, sasquatch." Hammer slapped him on the back.

"What?" When Razor finally realized what she meant, he was shocked because they hadn't been trying. "But . . . another one? So soon?"

"Yes. The doctor confirmed it this morning."

Razor's face lit up, and he leaned over and hugged her. He never imagined he'd be here with a family and friends. He'd come to terms with all his insecurities about his relationship with Eve. One of the first things he'd done when he'd decided to move back to Virginia was register with the Hampton VA Medical Center. Razor was talking to a therapist once a month. The nightmares had subsided, and the last one was over a year ago. His main focus had been taking care of Eve and helping with her recovery from what had happened. It had been a long and difficult road, but she was better physically and mentally. Razor made sure she got all the help she needed, which also included talking to her own therapist. Wyatt was a blessing, and to learn he was going to be a father again made Razor the happiest he'd ever been. "I love you, Eve."

THE END

Kimberly A. Biggerstaff © 2025

If you or someone you know is in crisis and needs immediate help, visit the National Institute of Mental Health (NIMH) at nih.gov.

NIMH does not monitor the website or the emails or phone numbers listed on the website for crisis messages, provide medical advice, or make referrals.

If you are thinking about harming yourself or attempting suicide, tell someone who can help right away:

- Call 911 for emergency services.
- Go to the nearest hospital emergency room.
- Call or text **988** to connect with the 988 Suicide & Crisis Lifeline. The lifeline provides 24/7/365 confidential support to anyone in suicidal crisis or emotional distress. Support is also available via live chat. Para ayuda en español, llame al 988.

If you have a family member or friend who is suicidal, do not leave them alone. Try to get the person to seek help immediately from an emergency room, physician, or mental health professional. Take seriously any comments about suicide or wishing to die. Even if you do not believe your family member or friend will actually attempt suicide, the person is clearly in distress and can benefit from your help in receiving mental health treatment.

For information about the American Legion, please visit www.legion.org.

Additional Resources

The American Legion a U.S. Veterans Association

Be the One | The American Legion www.legion.org/betheone

The Columbia Protocol: About the Protocol - The Columbia Lighthouse Project

Kimberly A. Biggerstaff © 2025

If you need information about domestic violence, please contact <u>Domestic Violence Support | National Domestic Violence Hotline.</u>

www.thehotline.org

Call 1-800-799-SAFE (7233)

Text "START" to 88788

About the author

Kimberly Biggerstaff served honorably for nearly ten years in the United States Air Force as a Law Enforcement Security Policewoman (811X2, 3P0X1). She gives back to her fellow veterans by being an active member of one of the largest Veterans Service Organizations in America, the American Legion.

After leaving the service she obtained her teaching degree and taught special education. A full-time mom, Kimberly stays busy raising two special needs daughters and a dog with her husband.